RING OF DRAGONS

Ring of Dragons

(Age of the Sorcerers—Book Four)

Morgan Rice

MORGAN RICE

Morgan Rice is the #1 bestselling and USA Today bestselling author of the epic fantasy series THE SORCERER'S RING, comprising seventeen books; of the #1 bestselling series THE VAMPIRE JOURNALS, comprising twelve books; of the #1 bestselling series THE SURVIVAL TRILOGY, a post-apocalyptic thriller comprising three books; of the epic fantasy series KINGS AND SORCERERS, comprising six books; of the epic fantasy series OF CROWNS AND GLORY, comprising eight books; of the epic fantasy series A THRONE FOR SISTERS, comprising eight books; of the new science fiction series THE INVASION CHRONICLES, comprising four books; of the fantasy series OLIVER BLUE AND THE SCHOOL FOR SEERS, comprising four books; of the fantasy series THE WAY OF STEEL, comprising four books; and of the new fantasy series AGE OF THE SORCERERS, comprising five books (and counting). Morgan's books are available in audio and print editions, and translations are available in over 25 languages.

TURNED (Book #1 in the Vampire Journals), ARENA 1 (Book #1 of the Survival Trilogy), A QUEST OF HEROES (Book #1 in the Sorcerer's Ring), RISE OF THE DRAGONS (Kings and Sorcerers—Book #1), A THRONE FOR SISTERS (Book #1), TRANSMISSION (The Invasion Chronicles—Book #1), and THE MAGIC FACTORY (Oliver Blue and the School for Seers—Book One) are each available as a free download on Amazon!

Morgan loves to hear from you, so please feel free to visit www.morganricebooks.com to join the email list, receive a free book, receive free giveaways, download the free app, get the latest exclusive news, connect on Facebook and Twitter, and stay in touch!

SELECT ACCLAIM FOR MORGAN RICE

"If you thought that there was no reason left for living after the end of THE SORCERER'S RING series, you were wrong. In RISE OF THE DRAGONS Morgan Rice has come up with what promises to be another brilliant series, immersing us in a fantasy of trolls and dragons, of valor, honor, courage, magic and faith in your destiny. Morgan has managed again to produce a strong set of characters that make us cheer for them on every page.... Recommended for the permanent library of all readers that love a well-written fantasy."

—*Books and Movie Reviews*
Roberto Mattos

"An action packed fantasy sure to please fans of Morgan Rice's previous novels, along with fans of works such as THE INHERITANCE CYCLE by Christopher Paolini.... Fans of Young Adult Fiction will devour this latest work by Rice and beg for more."

—*The Wanderer, A Literary Journal* (regarding *Rise of the Dragons*)

"A spirited fantasy that weaves elements of mystery and intrigue into its story line. *A Quest of Heroes* is all about the making of courage and about realizing a life purpose that leads to growth, maturity, and excellence.... For those seeking meaty fantasy adventures, the protagonists, devices, and action provide a vigorous set of encounters that focus well on Thor's evolution from a dreamy child to a young adult facing impossible odds for survival....Only the beginning of what promises to be an epic young adult series."

—*Midwest Book Review* (D. Donovan, eBook Reviewer)

"THE SORCERER'S RING has all the ingredients for an instant success: plots, counterplots, mystery, valiant knights, and blossoming relationships replete with broken hearts, deception and betrayal. It will keep you entertained for hours, and will satisfy all ages. Recommended for the permanent library of all fantasy readers."

—*Books and Movie Reviews*, Roberto Mattos

"In this action-packed first book in the epic fantasy Sorcerer's Ring series (which is currently 14 books strong), Rice introduces readers to 14-year-old Thorgrin "Thor" McLeod, whose dream is to join the Silver Legion, the elite knights who serve the king…. Rice's writing is solid and the premise intriguing."

—*Publishers Weekly*

TABLE OF CONTENTS

CHAPTER ONE

Master Grey stood over Royalsport, arms spread wide as he held the tides of the city's rivers unnaturally high, feeling the great weight of all that was happening starting to bear down on him. He'd known that so much of this would come, known that there would be many deaths along the way, but the reality of it was worse, far worse.

A bead of sweat dripped down his face as he looked out over the city below, the darkness proving no impediment to him. He'd learned *that* secret long ago. Below, he could see Royalsport spread out, carved up into its separate districts by the onrush of the water, each now a small island unto itself. Across those islands, hundreds, if not thousands, of troops in the red and purple of King Ravin's men swarmed.

His magic had broken them up into separated groups, at least, and meant that the largest bulk of the forces was still trapped on the outskirts of the city, able to do no more than put a containing ring around Royalsport's exits. Another group was in the district where the House of Weapons usually belched smoke and flame even in the dark, but now its furnaces lay silent, the men there caught up in defense of it. More had spread into the other districts, around the Houses of Scholars, of Merchants, of Sighs. Cut off from one another, they might do less damage, but there was still plenty of harm they *could* do, and might, now that they had seen so many of their own washed away.

Master Grey winced at that thought; how many lives had he taken tonight, tumbling and broken along the riverbanks, or drowned in the depths? However many it was, they were more faces for the tally that the sorcerer kept within himself, and that some part of him knew would have to be paid someday. Eventually, all things came due.

All this to keep them from a rush on the castle that would have seen those within slaughtered as the soldiers gave way to bloodlust. In that, at least, Master Grey had succeeded. Below, he could see the group led by King Ravin trapped in the noble district near the castle, unable to progress.

A part of Master Grey wished that he could simply reach out and stop the man's heart with his magic. It would save so much suffering to come, but to do it would set too many other things in motion. He had to trust that the things that were already happening were sufficient, that the people involved were all that he hoped they would be. In any case, doing such things with magic twisted men too much. He was not one of the Hidden, to override the balance of things and become progressively more warped. He worked with that balance, and that was what gave him power.

As if to remind him of the limits of that power, Master Grey found his hands shaking, yet he maintained the spell, his mind holding in place all the delicate links of connection required to send water rushing where it should not. Every second he held this was one in which those within the castle could prepare more, and that events could progress along the paths given to them. Master Grey thought of Devin, sent to collect the fragments of the unfinished sword; of Erin, fighting down below in the alleys; of the figures yet to play their parts in all of this.

For now, his part was simple: he had to hold on. Second by second, though, minute by minute, it was getting harder. Sooner or later, he would fail, and then...then the storm of violence would follow.

King Ravin stared up at the tower that stood off to the side of the castle. The sorcerer stood there atop it, and for a moment, Ravin was sure that the man was looking his way. That was good; let him see the enemy who was coming for him, and for all of them.

Around him, the buildings of the noble district stood quiet and dark, the inhabitants within too frightened to come into the streets. They had good reasons to be afraid: around Ravin, the bodies of those who had stood in his way lay hacked down, still in death. Before, the enemy's soldiers had tried to block their advance into the district, but now, only his own men stood there. They owned the streets here, the men waiting in silence for his commands.

"What do you require of us, my king?" one of his officers asked. "Do we continue to the castle?"

Ravin considered it; he was sure that at least some of his men would throw themselves into the water of the castle's moat if he commanded it, and if he'd had his full forces there, maybe he would have considered it, bridging the gap with the sheer weight of numbers. He had only these few, though, and in any case, there was no need.

Ravin was no magus, but he had learned about magic and its limits, the same way he had learned all the other weapons that a king might gain access to. Master Grey was undoubtedly powerful, but he was still a man, still had limits.

"The spell will fall eventually," Ravin said, keeping his voice calm, showing his troops that this setback was not a problem. "Work to reconnect the districts. Throw ropes between houses so that men can clamber over and carry messages. Contact the men we have in each district."

"Yes, my king," the man said, nodding to some of the men there and sending them running off to fulfill the orders.

Ravin thought about what the wizard was trying to do. To another man it might have seemed obvious: cut off pockets of troops and let defenders pick them apart. Yet to Ravin, that didn't make sense. There were not enough troops still in the city to make something like that work. Instead, all that would happen was that the invasion would be slower.

What else, then? Perhaps the man was hoping that Ravin would panic and withdraw, or perhaps he was hoping that if he only held on long enough, the defenders would be able to prepare enough to hold the castle. Perhaps his only thought was to protect the castle. Not everyone thought as deeply about strategy as Ravin did, maybe not even sorcerers.

Perhaps his strategy would have worked if Ravin had not prepared so carefully, or if he had been a less patient commander. Perhaps it might have worked if Ravin had not been able to get clear of the stream bed in time, too. When fighting for a crown, killing the man who sought to wear it was an effective way to win.

It was also something Ravin would not forgive. The sorcerer would die for that attempt on his life. But not yet.

"Spread out," he told the others. "One of you find a high point and signal the others with your torch. Tell the rest of the men to do the same. I want them to hold the city, make it ours. Crush any resistance, and anyone on the streets is fair game, but do not destroy more than you need to."

"Where will you be, your majesty?" the officer asked.

"Follow me."

Ravin picked a noble household at random, choosing one with elegantly scrolling stonework around the door, and plants set in the windows that trailed down like tears for the dead in the city. He stepped up to the door and hammered a fist against it. Understandably, only silence answered him.

Ravin raised one booted foot and kicked the door, shattering the bolts that held it with a single blow. He stepped into a hallway where paintings hung, depicting figure after figure in what he assumed was a statement about the owner's ancestry and his right to all they owned. Ravin was still looking at them when a man came at him out of the dim light of the house, rushing at him with a sword raised. Ravin struck it aside, and then hacked his own sword through the man's chest, so that he tumbled to the ground at Ravin's feet.

"If you had started off there, you would have lived," he said.

He stalked through the house, to the spot where a kitchen sat, following the only flicker of light that he could see within the place. He pushed open the door there and found a woman and what he assumed were her daughters huddled at the back of the kitchen, along with a knot of servants. They huddled near the fire, trying to use a large wooden table tipped on its side as a kind of barricade. A couple of serving men had knives in their hands, stepping forward as if they might fight.

Ravin raised his sword, the blade still wet with the blood of the man who had come at him.

"Do you really think you can best me?" he demanded. "I am Ravin, King of the Three Kingdoms, your rightful ruler. Kneel, or die."

He put the full force of his command into his voice, and he watched the men pale as they understood the enormity of who they faced. The knife of one rattled to the floor, but the other was slower. Ravin's patience left him, and he thrust his sword home in that man's chest, ignoring the screams of the women around him. Ravin kicked him back, then pushed the table back over onto its feet. He took a chair, putting it before the table and setting his still bloody sword down on it.

He looked around at those of his men who had followed him in. "I will be here. Go about your duties."

They set off, only a couple remaining behind as his bodyguards. Ravin sat there, considering those left living in the room. All were on their knees now, looking up at him with obvious terror.

"One of you bring me wine," he said. "The rest of you consider one simple fact: everything that you thought was yours is mine now—your coin, your property, yourselves. This city, this whole *kingdom*, is mine."

Or it would be, just as soon as the magus's spell fell away.

CHAPTER TWO

The great hall of the castle was a hive of activity, its squares of carpet overrun with people rushing back and forth about whatever task they could find, the high stone walls ringing with their conversations as they tried to work out what to do next.

To that extent, it reminded Lenore of the buzz of activity in the weeks before her wedding, when the whole castle had been filled with festivities, but there was nothing light or joyous about things now. Instead, some of the banners around the walls had been pulled down, nobles currently arguing over whether they should be cut to make makeshift bandages, while the throne sat empty, with no sign of Vars to fill it, and the man who *should* have sat there dead.

Just the thought of that filled Lenore with grief, but she found herself having to pretend to be calm, having to be the still center around which others were able to turn. They needed someone who was in control, poised, and who thought when they merely wanted to act; they needed a princess, and that meant that Lenore was playing the part she had been preparing for her whole life.

"No," she said, "don't just barricade the great hall's outer door; I want the pieces nailed in place."

"But where are we to find nails?" a nobleman asked. Lenore took no pleasure in the fact that he was looking to her for instructions when just a day or two before he might have seen her as some pretty, useless ornament.

"I don't know. Search the castle's stores if you have to," Lenore said. "*Go.*"

The man went without question. Quite a lot of those there were acting without questioning her instructions. Lenore suspected a lot of it had to do with who she was: the sister of the new king and the wife of Duke Viris's son. Possibly some of it also had to do with people simply wanting someone to tell them what to do now that there was a crisis.

Lenore found herself wishing that there was someone who could tell *her*.

She was as frightened right then as she had ever been in her life. There was an army in the city, composed of people like the ones who had kidnapped her. The Knights of the Spur were gone, and so were most of the soldiers. How were they supposed to hold out against all of that? If the castle fell, then what? Would everyone within be slain out of hand?

That wasn't even the worst thing Lenore could imagine, given the horrors that had happened to some of her maids during the kidnapping. She had only been in one battle, and that had been terrifying enough, but what would it be like when a whole horde of out of control soldiers descended on the castle?

Then there was King Ravin, the man who had ordered her taken, the man who was responsible for the death of her brother and her father. Lenore had heard the stories about his cruelty, each one more sickening than the last. Just the thought of him made fear crawl down her spine.

"Your highness," a servant said. "Do you want weapons brought here from the armory?"

Lenore considered her potential troops. There were servants who had probably never held a sword in their lives. There was a scattering of nobles, many of whom were older, and most of whom looked just as afraid as Lenore felt. Even so, maybe it was better to at least try to put up a fight. Even dying quickly like that might be better than the alternatives.

"Fetch what you can for people," she said. She pointed to another servant. "Go with him."

"Yes, your highness," the man said.

Lenore continued to organize what she could of the defenses for the castle, turning to servants and nobles in turn. "You, take whoever you need and go to the kitchens to find whatever oil you can. Take it to the gatehouse and start to heat it, ready to pour down. You, close the gates and drop the portcullis."

"What about those out in the city?" the man asked.

Lenore's heart broke at the question, and at the answer to it that she didn't want to say. "They...with the waters high, there is no chance for them to get back. If we see them return we can...we can drop ropes."

She didn't say what the odds were of them returning; she wouldn't think about it, because Erin and that strange monk of hers were still out there, fighting the enemy. Perhaps they were even safer out there than in the castle, because it meant that they would have a chance to hide and run when the time came. Not that Erin would ever willingly run, but maybe Odd would make her.

Lenore looked around, knowing that she and the others there wouldn't have a chance to run. Their only hope was to try to hold the castle, and the truth was that they had too few people to do it. She could give every servant a spear, insist that every noble line up on the walls to try to fend off the oncoming tide, and it still wouldn't be nearly enough. The tasks that she was setting people were more because she knew they needed to feel useful at a time like this than because she truly thought it would do any good when King Ravin's army came.

Perhaps it might have helped if she actually knew more about strategy. Currently, everything she had commanded was some half remembered fragment gleaned because Erin had insisted on playing at defending the place from imaginary foes when they'd been little, or because Rodry or their father had told stories of how they had fought against this enemy or that. Some of it had seemed obvious, but too much of it wasn't.

She wished for what felt like the hundredth time that someone else were here to take charge of things. Vars was supposed to be king now, but he wasn't here to command. Rodry and her father were both gone, dead right at the moment when they all most needed their skills in war. Erin was out in the city, doing what she could in the place where it might help most. Even as Lenore understood the sense of it, understood that with so few troops, hitting and running in the city was better than waiting in the castle, she wished that her sister were there beside her.

She even found herself wishing for Finnal, even though Lenore didn't know *what* to think about her husband. Was he the good man that he seemed sometimes, or the cruel one that he seemed at others? In a bard's tale, this would be the moment when he came running in to take command of it all and prove to Lenore just how much he loved her. Instead, there was no sign of him. Maybe he was off playing his part in the defense of the city?

Even more than Finnal though, Lenore found herself wishing that Devin was there. He was clever, and kind, and every time she thought of him she felt...she felt *safe*. Maybe if he were there, there would be some trick that he'd learned from Master Grey, some way that he could help keep them safe. Even more than her husband, Lenore found herself long-ing for his presence. Maybe it was just as well that he wasn't there, though. Maybe it was better that he was off in the world, undertaking whatever strange task the sorcerer had set him. He would be safer there, perhaps. Certainly safer than Lenore was here.

Lenore was still considering that when her mother strode into the room. The striding was what caught her attention first; for so many of the days before, Queen Aethe had walked around like a hunched and broken thing. Now, though she still wore mourning black, she walked with the command of a general into the center of the room.

"Who is in charge here?" she demanded. All eyes looked Lenore's way.

"I think...I think I am, Mother," Lenore said.

Her mother put a hand on her shoulder. "Then you should not have to do this alone. You," she said, pointing to a nobleman. "Why are you standing idle? Find something useful to do, even if it's just cutting those banners to make bandages."

She'd obviously seen what Lenore had in mind for them, although she hadn't been there for that argument.

"But the banners," the man said. "They bear the royal crest."

"Do you think my husband cared more about banners or about the people carrying them?" Queen Aethe snapped back. "I'm the wife of one king and the stepmother of another. If one man bleeds to death because we didn't have enough bandages, I'll hold *you* responsible."

The nobleman hurried off about his task. Lenore could only stare at her mother.

"I spent ages trying to get them to do that," she said.

"Yes, well, they're more used to me being harsh," Queen Aethe said. She looked Lenore in the eyes. "As I was harsh with you over Finnal. A mother should be there for her daughter, and not just when she is doing what she thinks she ought to do."

After the last time they had spoken, when her mother hadn't listened, had thrown her grief in Lenore's face as if her own difficulties could never matter in the face of it, this was the last thing that Lenore had expected.

"Thank you," Lenore said, covering her mother's hand with her own.

"You shouldn't have to thank me for behaving as a mother should," she said. "You were right before, when you told me that there was more in the world than just my grief."

"I'm sorry," Lenore said. "I was harsh when I said it. I miss Father too."

"I know," Queen Aethe said. "But you were right. There are bigger things. His kingdom, *our* kingdom, is in danger, and I will not stand by. I will do what is required to protect it, and you. *Whatever* is required."

Chapter Three

Erin knelt poised atop a wall, watching with revulsion as three of King Ravin's soldiers passed below. In the darkness of the early morning, they couldn't see her, and it was probably just as well. Erin had never cared much about her appearance, always hacked her dark hair short to keep it out of the way and worn tunics and hose instead of dresses where she could. Now though, she looked like a monster.

It wasn't just the blood covering her armor, or the dents in it from where enemies had gotten in blows. There was also the dirt, carefully smeared over her armor and face to help her blend into the dark. More than that though, there was everything she felt. Odd might have spent his time trying to teach her to fight with serenity, but right then all Erin could feel was rage at the men who had invaded her home.

She leapt down from the wall, shouting with that anger as she led with her spear, plunging it into the first of the trio of soldiers. More blood joined the patina of it on her armor, spurting up as she impaled her foe. She hit the ground hard and rolled to her feet, abandoning her spear momentarily in favor of a long knife clutched in either hand.

The two remaining soldiers were turning to her by then, but caught in their shock at the attack, they were slow, and Erin was already in close to the second, stabbing with both short blades, too close for him to bring his sword to bear.

She kept the dying man between her and the third, using him as a shield to block the blow of an axe. She let her already dead foe fall, dragging his comrade's axe with him, and it turned out that the final man had looped his axe around his wrist with a length of cord so that he wouldn't drop it in the middle of battle. It meant that he was bent over and exposed as Erin lunged in, slamming a knife into the side of his neck.

How many was that now? At the start of the night, Erin had tried to keep track of the numbers, even tried to make a game of it with the men who followed her. Now though, she had lost track; there had simply been too many for that.

It was a long way from the games of chivalry she'd sometimes persuaded Rodry to play with her when she'd been little; a long way even from the kind of swift, righteous violence she had meted out back in the village that had been taken by Ravin's Quiet Men with Sir Til and Sir Fenir. This was gritty, house to house, hitting and running, killing and fading back into the shadows.

Erin went to retrieve her spear, putting a foot on the first soldier's back and pulling until it came free with an ugly, wet sound. She was just cleaning the worst of the gore from it when she heard the sound of booted feet approaching, and saw what had to be another twenty of Ravin's troops lit by lamplight, approaching fast.

"Damn it," she swore and set off running. Behind Erin, the footsteps sped up to match, and now it was a race, turning left and right, Erin hoping she knew the streets of Royalsport as well as she thought she did. Yes, this was the Street of Potters, and *this* was the alley where on better days they threw their waste clay. Erin knew where she was.

That didn't make her any safer. A crossbow bolt flashed past her shoulder, setting her darting in zigzags as she ran, not wanting to present any enemy with a still target. She leapt over a stack of boxes, heard figures behind her crash through them, and put in a sprint to keep ahead of them.

She was tired, and not just from the running. A dozen small wounds marked her by now from fights earlier in the night. She'd been awake for more hours than she could remember, and then there was the endless, numbing violence of it all, with men dying around her at every step, friend and foe both.

Still, the battle rush carried her through, letting Erin take another turning into a courtyard that smelled as though it was behind a tannery, the stench an even greater assault on her nostrils than the blood. There was no obvious way out of the courtyard, so she turned at bay, watching as the soldiers came on, moving slower now as they realized that she had nowhere else to run.

"Now!" she called out.

Men clambered into view on the roofs, holding bows and crossbows, spears and even rocks at this stage. They started their barrage, firing down at the hemmed in enemy, while a few of them moved in behind, ready to cut off any attempt they made to escape. In an effort to break free, one of the men rushed at Erin, sword high. Erin barely stepped to the side in time, driving her spear up into his guts even as he missed her.

Her men dropped down then, following their initial volley with the violence of swords, clubs, and axes. They hacked at the Southern Kingdom's soldiers, killing one after another, but it wasn't without its cost. Erin saw one of the noble retainers who had come with her pierced by a short sword, saw a guardsman's head broken open by the impact of a mace. Every time she saw one of her people fall, Erin winced, feeling it as if it were her own flesh being destroyed. Yet she knew that this was the price of command; she couldn't keep all of the people who followed her safe. All she could do was hope that each one of their lives bought as many dead enemies as possible.

The fight in the courtyard was swift and brutal, King Ravin's soldiers dead in less than a minute. Erin and her men didn't stay around in its aftermath though, because there would be more coming. There were always more coming. Instead, they snatched what weapons they could from the dead and set off through the streets, sticking to the back ways, relying on the fact that they knew the city better than their foes.

"How many more?" a man asked behind Erin. She could hear his weariness, even shared it, but she knew she couldn't show it.

"As many as is needed to drive them out of our city," Erin replied. "We keep going. We don't stop. Everyone's lives depend on it." She was sure that her brother or her father, or even Lenore, would have had a rousing speech right then; all Erin could do was lead by example. "Get a rope strung up."

The man grumbled but nodded, heading up to one of the buildings nearest the next stream and flinging a rope across, tugging on it until he was sure it had caught a chimney stack on the other side. Erin's men tied off the near end on their roof, but *she* was the one to step out onto it, walking it as nimbly as an acrobat. Below, the usually placid river running

13

between the poorest district and the entertainment district was roaring like the Slate itself. Above, Erin could see the figure of Master Grey, still holding his spell.

"I know this slows the enemy, wizard, but it doesn't exactly make things easy for *us* either," she muttered as she landed lightly on the opposite roof. There, she saw that the tangle of the rope had almost slipped undone; another second or two, or had she been heavier, and Erin would have plunged into the waters. She tied it tightly, making sure that her men could follow. They hurried after her, stringing a second rope above the first so that they could cross more easily.

"The enemy look like they're having the same idea," one of them said as he crossed. "I'm sure I saw lamplight over the river."

"Where?" Erin asked, and scrambled up the side of a building until she saw a spot where it seemed that lights were too close to the river. She ran for it, hurrying through the alleys with the men following in her wake.

She slowed as she got closer, moving in the darkness. She found a rope bridge there between two buildings, a man moving across. He looked like a messenger, but it didn't matter to Erin what he was doing, only that he was involved in trying to murder the people of her city. Taking the head of her spear, she slashed with it, cutting one of the ropes in a single blow.

The man seemed to sense that something was wrong. He turned and started back for the far shore, but Erin was already slashing a second rope. She saw the shadow of the messenger fall into the water below, and Erin turned to the men who followed her.

"We can't allow this," Erin said. "But we can make use of it. We sneak up and cut their bridges with men on. We kill the ones who cross. If they have orders for the other groups in the city, we change them to lead them into traps. Everything they do, we'll find a way to make them pay for it with their lives."

"And what about our lives?" another of her men said.

"Do you want the truth?" Erin said. "Our lives don't matter right now. Think of all the other people in this city, all the ones who will die, or be little better than slaves, if the Southern Kingdom takes Royalsport. Their only hope is that we keep moving, keep killing as many of Ravin's men as we can."

Maybe she would even get lucky and find King Ravin with few enough troops around him that she could kill him. As the night wore on, though, it seemed less and less likely. No, it wasn't even night anymore. Above Erin, she could see a thin sliver of light on the horizon, red as any of the blood being spilled in the city streets. Ordinarily, she would have welcomed the dawn, but now she cursed it. Darkness was their friend and their protection; light was the last thing they needed.

Soon, Erin knew she would have to pull back to the castle; she hated the idea of leaving Lenore and their mother so unguarded for so long. For now, she had to try to keep fighting, even as the numbers of the Southern Kingdom's army seemed endless in comparison to their own small and splintered force.

"We're not done yet," Erin promised her soldiers. "Come on."

Spear in hand, she plunged into the early dawn light, looking for the next group of her enemies to kill.

CHAPTER FOUR

Odd cut at a soldier as the man came at him, timing the blow so that it struck aside his foe's attack even as the point sliced across his throat. At a sound beside him, he spun and parried another attack, kicking to send the man sprawling back, then cut at a third to force him to leap back out of the way of Swordmaster Wendros, unable to complete the thrust he was just lining up.

"Careful," Odd said. "That one almost had you."

"I knew you would get to him," the swordmaster replied, expertly disarming an oncoming soldier and then thrusting his own slender blade through the man's chest.

Around them, the training floor of the House of Weapons was awash with violence, the smiths and the teachers there fighting alongside one another as King Ravin's soldiers came at them to try to take control of its armories. Odd saw men fighting with hammers and with blades, using both their tools and the things they had crafted with them.

Here in the training ring where Odd and Swordmaster Wendros fought back to back, men clambered over the wooden railings that surrounded the space, coming forward at them in ones and twos to attack with everything from swords to halberds, spears to battleaxes. Odd deflected an arming sword to the left, striking with the pommel of his longsword to stun a foe and then all but decapitating him with a backhand sweep. One came in from the other side and Wendros beat the blade up as it headed for Odd, leaving the way open for Odd to cut the oncoming soldier down.

"You're very good," Wendros observed, moving with apparently effortless ease to avoid the sweep of an axe, killing the man who came at him with a flick of his blade. "From the rumors, I had assumed that you would be wilder."

Odd grunted a response, sinking into the space that he fought in now, calm precision taking the place of fury, so that his blade darted out once, then again, to pick off two more opponents.

"Is this really the time to have this conversation?" he demanded, as the sting of a blade across his arm brought him back to himself. He slashed out in response, felt the impact of his sword against flesh, but didn't have time to stop and see the results.

"That happened because you roll your wrist slightly too much as you go from your parry to your counter," Swordmaster Wendros said. As if to punctuate the point, he deflected a blade, and then thrust his own sword up through the roof of a man's mouth.

"If I want a sword lesson, I'll ask," Odd said. He ducked another blow, killed another man, and kept going.

There was something mechanical about the violence at this stage, so that instead of thinking about feint and counter, tactics and distance, there was only the movement and the killing, moving from one opponent to the next.

Even so, Swordmaster Wendros made it all look easy. He moved smoothly and with perfect timing, never seeming to hurry, just always seeming to be there when he needed to be. He deflected strikes and let them pass him, struck out with almost casual deadliness, and left a trail of bodies in his wake. Only the limp of his injured leg threw off his balance, slowing him down and lending a jerky quality to some of his footwork.

Even as Odd struck down another opponent, he couldn't help wondering just how good a swordsman the swordmaster must have been in his prime. Odd had always been considered one of the most dangerous of the Knights of the Spur, but the swordmaster was something else. It was a wonder Odd hadn't sought him out to fight him, really.

Odd sank deeper into the meditation of the violence, experiencing every moment so vividly that it seemed to fill his senses. All the colors of the place were brighter, the sounds of the battle clearer, each with its own message, so that he found that he could pick out the ebb and flow of the fight around him just from that. There were fewer small fights going on around them now, the participants fallen or victorious, Odd didn't know which. He could make out the breathing of the men coming at them, pick out every detail of a sword that came for his skull even as he avoided it, killing the man with an upward thrust.

In an instant, there were no more foes left to fight. The space around the training ring was empty of enemies, the space within only containing their corpses, the scent of death filling everything. Above, through broad, arching windows, Odd thought that he saw a thin sliver of dawn coming in shades of red.

"I never thought we would live long enough to see that," he said, looking over to Swordmaster Wendros. The man sat on one of the railings of the training ring, binding a wound on his torso with a strip of cloth. Odd hadn't seen the strike get through, hadn't believed that anything *could* get through the precise web of his defenses.

"Once, even this wouldn't have touched me," the swordmaster said, with an irritated sound. Odd could believe it.

"I would have liked to have fought with you back then," Odd said.

The swordmaster frowned. "I wouldn't," he replied. "I've heard about the man you were. We wouldn't have fought unless it was to the death."

Odd bowed his head, because he couldn't avoid the truth of that. Once, the pride in him wouldn't have let him stand for another man of that skill existing without trying him, and the battle rage wouldn't have let it be about anything but blood.

"I'm not the man I was," Odd said. It was more of a hope than a fact.

"Who among us is?" Wendros countered. "I'm honored to fight beside you now, though."

That caught Odd a little by surprise. Erin seemed pleased to be his student, but she didn't know the full reality of who he was and what he'd done. Swordmaster Wendros was old enough to know, but didn't shrink back from him the way most of the Knights of the Spur would have.

"So," Wendros said. "Is there a plan to all of this?"

"We help where we can," Odd said. "There are too many of the enemy, and too few of us. Princess Erin is leading men to hit and run in the streets. She sent me here to try to secure men and weapons for the fight."

There were few enough men left now, though. While the training rooms stood empty of the invaders, there were only a few of the weapons teachers and smiths left standing among the space, and most of them bore wounds.

"Go," Odd ordered them. "There are too few of you left to hold this House. Join the fight in the streets. Kill your enemies and move. *Go.*"

They went, obviously glad to have someone who sounded like he knew what he was doing to give them commands.

"We should probably join them," Wendros said. He hopped down from his perch on the rail, wobbling slightly on his bad leg.

"Soon enough," Odd replied. "Whenever you're ready."

"Don't try to pity me," the swordmaster replied, "or we really will be fighting."

Even so, they made their way across the House of Weapons much slower than the others, heading down into the spaces where the forges lay and moving toward the exit. The forges lay silent now, only a dim glow from them adding to the rising light of the dawn.

"Do you think we can win this?" Wendros asked him.

Odd shrugged. "Sometimes it's just about how long you fight, and how well."

They were still making their way to the exit when more of Ravin's men started to enter the House of Weapons. A couple came in first, and Odd cut them down easily, but more came after them, and more behind them. They poured into the House of Weapons, almost too many to count. Certainly too many for the two of them to fight. Even so, Odd weighed his sword in his hand.

"Planning to charge in again?" Wendros asked.

"No," Odd said. "We fight and retreat, using the forges for cover."

It was a good plan, and they started to back away together, edging toward a way out. The enemy advanced slowly at first, as if no one wanted to be the first to reach them. Then a man came forward, charging them, and Odd cut him down.

Men poured in after, coming at him and Wendros from every direction. Now there was no time for elegance, no time for skill to come into it. There was only time to hack and slash, giving ground pace by pace. So far, that was all right, because the forges were protecting the two of them as they fought side by side, but even a glance back told Odd that there was going to be a problem; the same problem that he and Erin had faced on the bridge. Past the forges, toward the exit they were heading for, the space opened out and their enemies would be able to surround them. Only this time, Odd very much doubted that there would be an army coming to save them.

"It's a problem," Swordmaster Wendros said, obviously having seen the same issue. His sword swept around to bind to an enemy's blade as he killed him. "But it is a problem with a solution, at least."

"What solution?" Odd demanded, cutting down another man, then another.

"I hold the ground while you escape," Wendros said. He deflected a strike, and kicked a soldier back into two others. It slowed them for a pace.

"What? No," Odd said, and not just because he didn't like the idea of running from any fight. The swordmaster had treated him like an equal, not like a rabid dog to point at his enemies and run from the rest of the time.

"Do you think I can run?" Wendros asked, even as he killed another man. "Go, Odd!"

"I...thank you," Odd said. He fell back, heading for the door. He couldn't help glancing back, though.

What he saw burned itself into him as surely as any of the other dark memories of his life. He saw Wendros moving in a blur of steel, only seeming to touch his foes, but the sharpness of his blade was enough to end them with just that touch. He wound around swords, and bound to them, and killed the men who came at him even as they started to pour around him.

If his injured leg hadn't slipped as he turned to deal with another of them, perhaps he could even have held them all. As it was, his balance gave way, just for an instant, leaving the briefest of openings.

A sword found it, and he stood transfixed, even as he managed to kill another man. A second sword came in, thrusting up under his armpit, joining the first. Odd watched the swordmaster die, killing the men who came at him even as he did it.

Then it was time to do the one thing he'd never done in all his years as a Knight of the Spur. He ran, with all the soldiers of King Ravin following.

CHAPTER FIVE

Master Grey felt the light of the dawn washing over him. On another day, the warmth of it might have been pleasant, but now it was a disruption. Magic was about balancing the forces of the world, and every change could disrupt that balance. Dawn felt like a buffeting wind pushing at the edges of his mind, knocking him this way and that, impossible to control.

"Just...a few...minutes...longer," Grey muttered through gritted teeth. He was the fulcrum over which the levers of the world moved, the hub of the wheel, the still point at the heart of it all.

But he wasn't still. He had been trembling with the effort of it all almost since he started, sweat soaking into his robes as he struggled to keep everything connected, keep the magic flowing through him.

Every moment a spell lasted, it became harder to maintain, the neat structures of the first instants decaying and becoming wilder as the forces within lashed this way and that. A novice's spell would collapse at that point, as so many of Devin's had when shaping the star metal. A skilled magus could adjust for a while, but Master Grey had been holding this effort for hours, adapting to every change, bringing it all back into the whole.

There came a point where even he couldn't hold it much longer, though, and now, Master Grey had a choice to make. He could hold out a little longer, push himself to the absolute limit, but eventually the pressure of it would make the spell collapse, and him with it.

And then...he would be too exhausted to escape, too spent to fight back as King Ravin's forces came in. If they captured him, what then? Master Grey was not arrogant enough to believe that he would give away no secrets in the hands of Ravin's torturers, that he would not give them help if they forced him to.

He could not allow that to happen. There were still things that needed to happen, still things that he needed to do, or all of the Three Kingdoms would be in danger from worse things than just King Ravin's forces.

He took a last look around the city. Bathed in dawn as it was, it didn't take the sight of a sorcerer to take in the spread of the Southern Kingdom's army. It filled all the lower quarters of the city now, and soon, it would spread even to the castle. He took in the rush of the water, the fury of it running through the channels that split the city. Grey thought of all those who had died, and who still might die. He could only hope that he had saved some through his actions. Maybe they would do something to make up for the deaths that would follow.

He let the spell fall.

It was like releasing the reins of a stallion that wanted to charge, the pent up power bursting out in a thunderclap that echoed over Royalsport, even as the fury of the water below started to ebb. The streams started to fall, water moving back out toward the sea after so long being built up and contained. The levels dropped, and soon Master Grey knew that Ravin's troops would be able to pour across, unstoppable when joined together.

He needed to go.

He went to the chest that he kept locked in his rooms, taking the contents. Then he stood there, drawing on his power, hoping that he still had enough strength for this. There were some arts of magic that Master Grey understood better than anyone alive. What he did next was one of them. He took that power and shaped it, so that mists filled the room, obscuring even the walls. Master Grey started to walk through those mists, through the places between, step by careful step.

In the tower room, the mists started to lift, drifting from the windows and burning away in the sunlight. They had lasted long enough, though, because when they lifted, Master Grey was gone.

Vars fled through the tunnels that led from the castle with all the speed of a hunted animal, tripping over himself and rising, not caring that his knees bruised on the hardness of the stone. Right then, all that mattered was to be away, to get clear of it all.

He was filthy now from the dust and the dirt of the tunnel, his royal clothes torn from where they'd scraped on the floor, his dark hair streaked with dirt, his features smeared with dust. There were sections where the tunnel was tight, and Vars was glad he wasn't as broad or as tall as his brother Rodry had been. But then, Rodry wouldn't have been down here; he would have stayed to fight.

Fear fueled him, pushing him forward, lending him speed that his legs wouldn't have possessed at any other time. He knew that King Ravin would kill him for the throne, to make it clear that he had conquered the kingdom and to remove a rival at the same time. Vars cursed himself for his fear, even as it proved to be a blessing, letting him escape, letting him survive. Every step felt like a stride closer to safety, but also like he was abandoning his duties, running from all the things that he'd worked so hard to hold.

His father wouldn't have run; his brother wouldn't. Of course, both of them would only have died. Vars had done everything he could as king, had sent his forces to counter the threat posed by the Southern Kingdom. What more could anyone have done?

Ahead, Vars saw a chink of light and headed for it, finding a grate there that was fastened from the inside with bolts that were brown and red with rust. Vars hauled at them with all his strength, wishing in that moment that he'd spent more time strengthening his body the way Rodry had always said he should. He felt the metal bite into his hands, but he kept going, pulling at the bolts until the metal shrieked, and finally gave, tumbling him to the ground as the grate clanged open.

Vars stood and pulled himself up into the light of the dawn, gasping in the open air.

He came up and looked around, trying to work out where he was. Somewhere in the entertainment district, he thought, because he recognized the silk-swathed outline of the House of Sighs rising above the rest of it.

It was better than being in the castle, but he still needed to get out of the city.

Vars set off along the streets, keeping his head down, pulling back into doorways every time he heard the sound of soldiers coming. He saw them marching past in formation, asserting ownership of the streets as much as trying to do anything that was militarily useful. He saw a commoner in their path try to turn and run; they cut him down without hesitating.

Vars swallowed at that, knowing that they would do the same to him if they saw him, but thankfully they moved past, letting him keep going, on toward the outskirts of the city. The tremendous wash of the streams had receded, so Vars clambered across a mud-caked bed, keeping low and making for the walls.

He knew he couldn't try to make it through the gates, but there were always other ways in and out of a city. He'd used them sometimes when meeting with women, meeting with Lyril. Vars wondered what had happened to the noblewoman who had wanted to marry him so badly since he'd sent her away from him. Probably she was cowering in a house somewhere; that or trying to seduce some Southern officer. She'd always been good at trying to survive.

Vars could see the walls ahead now, and the spot where a small glover's shop lay, almost up against them. He looked both ways along the street, making sure there were no soldiers to be seen, and then sprinted for the cover of the shop.

He slid around behind it, to a space where an opening in the wall stood covered by wooden planks. It had long been used by smugglers, and Vars had been only too happy to turn a blind eye in exchange for the use of it when he needed to come and go discreetly. And the occasional small "gift," of course. Now, it would be his lifeline. All he had to do was get through it, find a horse on the other side, and ride out into the safety of the countryside. He would go into hiding until he could work out a way back to some sort of power.

Vars hunched down and pushed his way through the gap, moving quickly, not wanting to be seen. He pushed aside the covering on the other side; he'd done it! He was safe!

Rough hands grabbed him then, dragging him from the gap out into the open air. They flung him down onto the ground, and beside him, Vars could see half a dozen corpses lying in a pile where they'd been tossed. He rolled to his back and looked up into the faces of a pair of King Ravin's soldiers, terror running through him as he realized that they'd obviously been set to cover this weakness and kill anyone who tried to escape.

In a moment like that, Rodry, or even Erin, would probably have fought. Lenore would no doubt have died with dignity, Greave probably while quoting something poignant that people would talk about for centuries. Vars wasn't any of them. Instead, as a sword rose above him, he did the only thing he could think of: he raised his hands in surrender.

"My name is King Vars of the Northern Kingdom," he said. "And I am a hundred times more useful to King Ravin alive than dead!"

CHAPTER SIX

Greave rushed along the harbor that lay beyond the city of Astare, his dark hair caught by the sea breeze, his almost feminine features a bit roughened by days of dark beard, his clothes stained by travel and by violence. He tried to hold back the pain of loss that he felt as he looked around at every step, trying to find a boat that would carry him to safety even as the city above rang with the sounds of invasion.

There seemed to be no obvious candidates now. The ships of the Southern Kingdom stood guard around the largest of the ships there, admitting no escape for those, while small vessels moved away, scattering to the ocean. That meant that there were few of those left now, their captains taking their chances with the sea rather than sit there and wait for King Ravin's men to find them. Greave couldn't blame them. Perhaps... perhaps he should have simply gone on the boat that he'd sent off with Aurelle, and worked it all out afterward.

No. Just the thought of Aurelle made Greave's heart feel like it would burst with pain. When she'd come with him on this journey, he'd thought that it was because she loved him, the way that he had loved her. Greave had been so deeply wrapped up in her that he hadn't seen until it was far too late what she was: a spy sent to keep him from finding the hidden cure to the scale sickness, even if it meant killing him. It didn't matter that she'd helped him in the end; the betrayal... it hurt too much to simply let go.

Greave's hand went to the spot within his tunic where he'd hidden the page he'd torn from Hillard's notes, the parchment kept safe even while the rest of Astare's underground library had burned at Aurelle's hand. If he could just get to safety, just find the ingredients he needed...

Right then, though, Greave couldn't see a boat left that might carry him to safety. There were a few, but they were clearly too big for one man to handle, even if he'd known much about sailing. Worse, there were soldiers descending along the cliff path that led down to the docks, spreading out among them, moving as if they were searching for something.

Greave tried to force himself to be calm. It couldn't be for him. The men who had come after him and Aurelle in the great library were dead, either slain by Aurelle directly, or trapped by the fire they'd set there as they left. It still pained Greave to have been part of so much destruction in a place that held so much knowledge, but there was nothing he could do to change that now.

He made his way out to the last of the jutting wooden quays, hoping that there would be at least one captain still left who might help him. There was no one, though, and no boats that he could try to steal, risking his limited nautical skills against the tides. There were only stacks of supplies waiting for whatever ships came to the harbor next, or perhaps abandoned by ones that had run: barrels of tar, crates of hard tack, boxes of salt fish.

Greave turned to go back along the docks, determined to blend in and find a way out of Astare, but even as he did, he saw the soldiers who had come to the docks talking with the few inhabitants left there. He saw one point in his direction.

"No," Greave said. "They *can't* be looking for me."

It seemed that they were, though. Perhaps someone had made it clear of the burning library after all, or perhaps someone had spotted him and Aurelle on the streets and recognized him. Whatever it was, it meant that Greave was in terrible danger... and now there was no Aurelle to protect him.

Greave laughed bitterly at that thought, at wishing for someone who had hurt him so badly simply because she had proven herself dangerous with a knife. Still, didn't the philosopher Serecus write that love mattered less than the things that were practical in life? Didn't Yerrat write that it was better to have a strong enemy by your side against a mutual foe than weak friends? Greave always thought that one had lost something in the translation.

There was no point in wishing for Aurelle now, though, whether it was in the memory of the softness of her skin or just because she could kill a man quicker than Greave could blink. She was gone, her passage paid for, the captain sworn not to turn around. Greave had to make his own way out of there. He started back down the dock he was on.

He was too slow, too caught up in thoughts of Aurelle to move as quickly as he should. Even here, it seemed that she hurt him. The soldiers who had been asking after him were at the end of the dock now, and at least one had singe marks on his uniform that said he must have escaped the library fire.

"There's nowhere to run to, *Prince Greave!*" the man called out. "Oh, we know it's you, and the ways we're going to hurt you for trying to burn us before we give you to King Ravin, you're going to wish you never left Royalsport!"

Greave started to back away down the docks, the soldiers following at the leisurely pace of men who knew that their quarry had nowhere to run. The problem was that they appeared to be right. Greave thought through all the things he'd read on the tactics and strategies of the great commanders, all the games of strategy that he'd played that it was said would help a general learn to command. None of them seemed to have an answer for a situation where it was one man who knew nothing of swordplay, facing what looked like at least twenty men, with nowhere to run.

What would Aurelle do? The thought came to Greave sharp and unexpected, and a part of him wanted to push it down just because of how much it hurt to think of the red of her hair or the deep green of her eyes. But right now, *that* wasn't the part of her he needed to think about. He needed the ruthless woman who had been under the surface, the one who had set fire to the great library of Astare just so that they could…

That was it.

Greave continued to back away, keeping going until he was level with the barrels of tar. With a heave of effort, he tipped one over, sending the contents pouring out along the quay. He took flint and steel from his belt, and saw the eyes of the soldiers widen.

"You wouldn't," the one in front said. "You'll be killed."

"Actually," Greave said, "I suspect that with the wind in this direction and the fuel flowing away from me, there's a good chance I'll survive this. You, however..."

He struck sparks with his flint, letting them fall onto the tar. It roared up in response, and Greave had to throw himself backward onto the end of the dock as the blaze shot out. In seconds, it had hold of the dock, and more than that. Those of the soldiers who couldn't get out of the way fast enough fell screaming, trying to put out the blaze as it ate at them.

The fire shot along the dock, catching more of the barrels of tar. Greave felt the whole thing shudder as they exploded with the heat of it, more flames going high into the air. The dock lurched as its timbers split under the strain, and Greave had to struggle to hold his balance.

The heat of the fire was immense, like the roar of a forge on a summer's day. It claimed the supplies along the dock with the greed that only fire could have, and a part of Greave's mind dredged up all that he had read on the properties of flames, the ways in which scholars had theorized that such things could be drawn from the air with nothing more than fuel and sparks. None of it seemed like enough to account for the way the fire was eating its way along Astare's harbor, heading for the other docks now, spreading with such speed that Greave saw soldiers unable to run out of the way.

The fire on the dock was no less intense, its timbers shifting as the flames consumed the glue and rope that held them. Greave had a moment to wonder if maybe this had been the most well calculated of plans after all, and then he was falling, tumbling into the shocking cold of the water.

Spars and slats of wood tumbled down through the water around Greave like rain, so that it seemed as though one might strike him at any moment, yet none did. Greave held his breath, and tried to hold back his fear of the things that might be lurking there. He'd seen firsthand just how dangerous the creatures of the deep waters could be, could only hope that here near the docks there would be nothing so dangerous. Even under the water, he could feel the heat of the flames above him, see the flickering light of the fire as it seemed to spread out to fill the world.

When his lungs could take it no longer, Greave surfaced.

The harbor now was hellish, everything Greave could see aflame, even the large ships by the docks having to turn and run for open water to avoid damage. One was not fast enough, and Greave saw the fire climb its rigging like a candlewick, setting light to its sails so that they blazed above. He looked around, trying to find some way out of the inferno.

A whole section of the dock lay atop the water like a raft, a square of wood perhaps twice as long as a man on each side. In the water around, some of the barrels that had been abandoned floated. Greave swam over to them, thinking, trying to work out how many he would need. Slowly, with painstaking care, he started to push them into position under the broken section, lashing them into place with whatever rope was already there.

It took long minutes, but no one's attention was on Greave right then. When he was sure that he had done all he could, he clambered onto the makeshift raft, grabbing a section of wood to use as an oar. The raft wobbled but held, and Greave started to paddle from the harbor. He wasn't sure how far he would get like this, or how much control he would have once the currents took him, but it was better than here. He still had the method to make the cure, and all he had to do was find the ingredients.

Astare burned behind him as he left, but even so, Greave set off with hope in his heart.

CHAPTER SEVEN

"Take me back!" Aurelle insisted to the captain of the small vessel carrying her out of Astare. "Please, I can't leave Greave alone. He'll die there."

It made no difference, as all her other pleas had made no difference. The captain was a big man with a stony face that didn't show much, but now he smiled.

"*He'll* die without *you* there to protect him?"

The crew around Aurelle laughed, and that just made the mess of hurt and grief and shame inside her roil even more. Of course, she knew what they saw when they looked at her, the same thing she'd been so careful to project since the moment she met Greave. Her red hair might be whipping free rather than caught up in some elaborate noble braid, but they still saw her noble clothes, the sharp elegance of her features, the slenderness of her frame, everything down to the simple fact that she was a woman. All of that made them assume that she was someone who was weak, helpless.

She stepped back from him, trying to work out a way to do this, to get back to Greave, to just *explain* things. Everything would be all right, if she could just show him … if she could just show him that she loved him.

She clung to the rail of the boat, trying to work out if she could somehow swim back to Greave, but it was too far now, and in any case, the large ships of the Southern Kingdom would probably stop her before she got halfway.

She had to find another way, and the House of Sighs had taught her plenty of ways.

She watched the workings of the boat, trying to work out if there was some way she could make it happen by accident. She watched half a dozen men moving in concert to try to make it run smoothly, but it was clear that there was no way to turn it around without their aid. What next, then?

She waited until the moment when the captain headed belowdecks for a moment or two, then slipped into the space behind him, following him, trying to judge how best to do this. What would she do to get back to Greave? More to the point, what *wouldn't* she do?

"Are you here to try to get me to turn my boat around again?" the captain asked as she approached.

"I am," Aurelle said. "I need to get back to my prince. I'll do anything to get back. Anything."

She moved closer to the captain.

"Do you really think this is going to work?" he asked.

Aurelle drew a knife and pressed it against the captain's throat in one smooth movement.

"Take me back, right now," she said.

"Kill me, and my men will kill you," the captain said. The worst part was that it was probably true. With enough places to hide, Aurelle could have picked off all of the men there, but in the small space of the boat, she would be fighting six men head on. Even a Knight of the Spur probably couldn't have done that, and she was no knight. It was always better to put a knife in a back than to fight openly.

Even if she somehow managed to kill them all, that would leave no way to turn the boat around. Aurelle couldn't pilot it back to the harbor alone.

"*Why* won't you turn it back?" she demanded.

The captain shrugged. "I'm loyal to the crown, and I'm loyal once I'm paid. Prince Greave paid me to take you all the way to Royalsport, and so that's what I'll do."

"But he'll die there," Aurelle said. "We have to save him. I...I love him."

"My men probably didn't hear anything you and the prince said to each other," the captain said, "but I did. I know who you are. I know *what* you are, my lady, and I've no time for that kind of deception. I'll take you back, and you're lucky that we don't just cut your throat and throw you over the side for betraying the prince."

He went back up on deck, and it took Aurelle a moment before she felt able to follow, the sheer shock of her failure keeping her in place for a moment. She'd been so sure that she would find a way to turn this boat around, sure that she could find a way to manipulate the world to do anything she needed. Now, she was stuck. With a sigh, she went back up on deck.

There, she saw the docks of Astare ablaze.

"No!" Aurelle cried out as she saw it, taking in the burning ships, the wood of the dock front aflame. She saw a solitary figure standing on the burning end of one of the docks, and she saw it collapse from under him, fire seeming to consume the world around him. "No, please no."

Aurelle looked over to the captain, but he was just raising more sail, getting them away from Astare as fast as they could. There was no way he was going to turn now, no way he was going to take his boat back into flames that might consume it against Greave's express commands.

As she clung to the rail of the fishing boat, Aurelle could feel her heart breaking. She'd known that she felt more for Greave than she ever should have, more than was safe, or sensible, yet this...it could only hurt this much to lose someone when you loved them more than anything else in the world. At least, Aurelle assumed that was the case; she'd never loved anyone like this before.

In the House of Sighs, Aurelle had always prided herself on not being touched by anything as foolish as emotion. She'd seen all the ways that people tried to use one another, seen herself as being honest about the transactions at the heart of all things even as others tried to weave in stupid needs or feelings that only got in the way. When she'd been one of the ones chosen to spy, and act from the shadows, Aurelle had found it easy. It hardly felt like a betrayal when there was no love involved.

Now, it felt as though she had betrayed everything. She had betrayed Greave by spying on him in the first place, and she had betrayed everything she was supposed to be by daring to fall in love with him. Aurelle didn't know what to do.

She looked back at the blazing harbor, and right then it felt the way her heart did, everything aflame, so that soon, nothing would be left but ashes. Aurelle supposed that this kind of damage might hurt the Southern

Kingdom's invasion, but that was no kind of consolation. In any case, the fight in Astare was done; the city was theirs.

The worst part was that her employers would probably be happy with the way things had turned out. She could almost imagine the way Duke Viris would smile as she told him that the library that held the cure for scale sickness was burned, that the prince who had been searching for it was gone, along with the last page of the recipe.

Even if she tried to tell him that she hadn't done any of it, the duke would probably assume that she was merely being cautious, would be more than happy with the way things had turned out. Aurelle could imagine the way he would want to celebrate as well, because a man like that would never see her as anything other than a courtesan, however much she did for him.

Meredith... Aurelle knew that the mistress of the House of Sighs always acted in the interests of balance, of the kingdom, and of the House, that she always tried to protect the women and men who served it. Aurelle couldn't blame her for taking the duke's money, knowing that if Aurelle succeeded it would give the House of Sighs influence with him.

She could blame Duke Viris, though, and that son of his. He probably thought that Aurelle was stupid, and hadn't been able to see any of his plans. The desire to destabilize the royal family while simultaneously pushing Finnal higher and higher was so obvious, when viewed knowing what was happening. The fact that men like him so often thought that was at least one reason the House of Sighs was so good at what it did.

Greave didn't... Greave *hadn't* thought that way, and that thought was enough to send fresh pain through Aurelle. He was the one person who had ever loved her for who she was, not what she could do for them. The only person who had ever loved her, and now he was gone.

Aurelle stood there, feeling utterly bereft as Astare receded into the distance. She didn't know what she was going to do now, or where she was going to go once she got back to Royalsport. She didn't *want* to just tell Duke Viris that he'd succeeded, that all his plans were coming to fruition.

She realized what she wanted to do instead, and it was stupid, and dangerous, and would probably land her in more trouble than she could hope to survive. If she just went back and pretended that she'd done the job perfectly, she would be well paid, probably even able to maneuver herself into a position of power on the back of it.

Aurelle didn't want to do any of that. She couldn't stand the thought of a world in which Greave was gone, but the thought of one in which Finnal rose to power while Duke Viris smiled on in the background was like nails being dragged across her skin. She couldn't stand that thought... so why didn't she do something about it?

What she was contemplating wouldn't bring Greave back. It wouldn't undo any of the damage that she'd helped to do in the world, wouldn't make things right, but maybe, just maybe, it would make the world a better place.

She was going to kill them both.

CHAPTER EIGHT

The water battered Renard, throwing him around like a husband who had come back sooner than expected, so that he seemed to bounce from the water itself. He was a big man, but the water tossed him around like a toy, moving his weight as if it were nothing.

It caught at the cloak Renard wore, so that it became a lead weight around his shoulders. Renard tore at the garment, ripping it clear, but the clasp caught in the red of his hair, holding him in place as it snagged against a rock. Renard ripped a lump of his hair clear, and he came clear with it, thrown onward by the current.

Renard fought for the surface, trying to remember why it had seemed like such a good idea to throw himself into the water in the first place. He came up, managed to grab a breath, and remembered as he saw the great red bulk of the dragon lingering in the distance. Compared to being burned alive, what was a little water?

The river provided an answer to that as it dragged him back under, propelling him along with greater speed than Renard could ever have managed fleeing on horseback. He jolted against rocks, feeling them batter into his ribs, and had to use his arms and legs to push away from the worst of them before they could slam into him.

At least things couldn't get any worse.

He came up to the surface, and immediately regretted even thinking it. Ahead, the water gave way to froth and spray, while the river seemed simply to disappear beyond the spikes of a few rocks. A waterfall or a weir lay ahead, and Renard really didn't want to find out which by going over it.

He swam for the shore, not wanting to fight the river head on but dragging himself at an angle to it. Renard realized inside the first couple of strokes that it wasn't going to work. The river was too strong, pulling him too fast. Now Renard had to choose whether he was going to risk going over the edge or crash against the rocks that he could see—but then, recently, it seemed that his whole life had become that kind of choice.

Renard guessed that most people would have chosen the rocks, trying to cling to them to avoid going over the fall. They would probably have been dashed to death by them as a result, and Renard had never been one to cling to the safe option. He swam for the space between them, had a moment to see the space stretching out a hundred feet or more to the river below, and then he was falling.

Renard turned the fall into a dive as best he could, but even so, elegance didn't have much to do with the way he tumbled down into the waters that waited for him. There was the circle of a pool down there, and Renard just had to hope it was deep enough, or this fall was going to come to a sudden end.

He stretched out his hands, splitting the water apart as he hit it with an impact that still felt bone jarring. Renard arched back, trying to make his dive shallower, but even so, he felt himself hit the bottom of the pool hard enough to knock the remaining breath from him.

Above, Renard saw the surface as a circle of light that seemed far too far to reach out and touch. Renard's lungs were already starting to burn, and he had to fight not to take a breath as he set out toward the light.

It seemed to take forever to get there. Renard's vision started to darken, pressure building up inside his head until it seemed that it might explode. He was going to breathe soon whether he wanted to or not, and that would mean water pouring into him, drowning him...

Renard burst through the surface, gasping for air. He stared up, seeing the thundering waterfall high above him, and from down here it seemed even higher than it had when he was falling from it. Water hammered down around him, and right then it seemed like the most refreshing thing in the world to Renard, because it meant that he was alive.

"I'm *alive!*" he called out to the world in general, which was probably a stupid move. He'd already established to his own satisfaction that the gods were having far too much fun tormenting him. Renard set out swimming for the edge of the pool.

When he got to it, he hauled himself out of the water onto a stony bank, soaked to the skin and exhausted. He lay there for what felt like forever, the sun beating down hot enough now that it felt as though steam was rising from him.

Renard checked his possessions, trying to work out what had survived the trip downriver. He had no sword, but still had a long knife strapped to his hip. His coin pouch had survived, which meant he still had plenty of money thanks to the amulet he'd sold back in Geertstown.

Renard knew without looking that the amulet was still there. He could feel it, pulling at the edges of his being, sucking the life out of him little by little. Right then, Renard felt broken and bruised, exhausted and barely able to catch his breath. Even so, he could feel something far more insidious beneath it as the amulet started to pull the life from him.

Why wasn't he dead from it already? Renard wasn't normally someone to ask that kind of question, because it only seemed like an invitation for worse, but right then, he couldn't help but wonder. He could do nothing *but* wonder, since even with the prospect of a dragon somewhere back in the distance, possibly stalking him, he was too exhausted to move right then.

The fence he'd sold the amulet to had died less than an hour after he'd sold it, drained so completely that he'd barely looked human anymore. Yes, the man had been old, but even so, Renard couldn't believe that would be enough to make so much of a difference. There was something else going on, something he didn't understand.

Finally, Renard managed to push himself up to a sitting position, then to his feet. He knew without being told what he needed to do, had known it since the moment he'd stolen the amulet back in Geertstown: he needed the help of a sorcerer.

The problem was still the same. Sorcerers were anything but common, and finding someone who knew enough about magic to deal with an amulet that even the Hidden had been afraid of with all their terrible power ... how could he ever hope to find a man who could do that?

Renard started to walk, his clothes dripping water with every step. He'd gone a dozen paces before he even realized which way he was going.

The sun's position gave him the answer to that. He was heading east, in the direction of Royalsport.

He knew that was a stupid move, because all the rumors in Geertstown said that war was coming to the east. A town full of thieves and smugglers had felt like a safe haven compared to what lay in the rest of the kingdom.

Of course, quite a lot of Geertstown was currently on fire, thanks to the dragon that had come searching for the amulet.

Renard took it out now, staring at it. A sliver of dragon scale lay in the middle of an octagonal setting, each side bearing a different colored gemstone that shone in the sunlight.

"I should have left you behind," Renard said to the amulet. "When did *I* start going around doing the right thing?"

He had, though. He'd taken it back because of all the damage that might have come otherwise, and because the alternative had been leaving something this powerful in the hands of the Hidden. That motivation had already been enough to make Renard double-cross people who could tear him apart with magic.

One trip to Royalsport to find a sorcerer was nothing compared to that. He knew who he needed, because there was only one man who *could* help with something like this. Renard needed the help of the king's sorcerer, Master Grey. He needed to go to the wizard, even if that mean sneaking his way through whatever violence was out there to the east, and he needed to ask for his help.

Either that or just put the amulet in his hand and run, hoping that would be enough to break the connection there, and that the wizard would know what to do.

Either way, Renard kept walking, out over the rocky ground, keeping moving in the hopes of finding a road. When he found a trackway, he followed it until it led to a bigger trackway, and kept going.

He was all the way to the next village before he allowed himself to glance back, the thoughts of what might be lurking there keeping his eyes forward that long. Eventually though, Renard couldn't help himself. He looked over one shoulder, staring, searching the land and the sky.

It wasn't long until he found what he was looking for. It was no more than a dot now, but it was there, so that Renard knew he wouldn't be stopping at this village, or any other, for longer than it took to steal a horse.

The dragon hung there in the distance, following slowly, and Renard knew that if he didn't get to the sorcerer quickly, it would be burning him again, war or no war.

CHAPTER NINE

Nerra stared up at the great dark bulk of the dragon rearing over her, and she was sure that she was going to die. The deep, deep yellow of its eyes stared down at her, regarding Nerra as if trying to work out how easily it could devour her.

The evidence of the broken colony around her told her that it would take no more than a flicker of its breath to destroy her. Yet strangely, the thing that filled her heart most in that moment was not terror, but fascination.

Compared to the dragon whose egg she had found, this one was huge, and glossy and dark, but now, Nerra could see that the blackness was actually a dozen different shades and tints, from the lightest of grays to the deep black of tar, and the shadows of the night sky. Its scales were grown so broad that they were like armor plates on its underside, the only splashes of color on it the yellow of its eyes, and the deep red of the inside of its mouth as the dragon opened it wide.

It shot flame next to Nerra, and *that* pushed terror back into the forefront of Nerra's mind. She turned and ran, stumbling off through the wreckage of the ruined colony, heading for the trees rather than the rocky darkness of the open ground on the basis that nothing so large should be able to fit between them.

Nerra heard a roar behind her, and kept running.

Now she was in the jungle of the island's interior, the sun coming dappled through the canopy as she kept going. The plants flashing by Nerra as she ran weren't anything like the ones she knew back at home, lush and green, brightly colored and filling her nose with their scents. Was the overwhelming rush of them because they were truly that much more pungent, or was it about what she had become?

Above, even through the trees, Nerra could make out the shadow of the dragon flying overhead, huge and broad, keeping pace with her easily. Nerra couldn't help staring up at it, caught between her terror at the thought of such a huge predator above her and her appreciation of the elegance with which it cut through the air. It seemed to swoop and soar, barely flapping its giant wings, flame breathed at the air ahead to produce thermals that made its flight easier.

Wait, how did Nerra know that? She had seen her own dragon, of course, had felt a sense of connection to it, but she hadn't known anything about how their bodies worked or what it meant to *be* a dragon. Now, that knowledge just seemed to be there inside her, building up, impossible to ignore.

As she came out into a clearing, Nerra couldn't help staring up at the dragon, understanding as she did it the ways that its claws were almost as dexterous as hands, the way that its body could take magic from the air and turn it into flame, or shadow, or mist. She knew without being told that this dragon was female, and it was large even for its kind.

Nerra spent long seconds staring up at the dragon, and in those seconds, a flicker of movement came to her left. She saw something scaled and bestial spring from the trees, leaping forward at her with teeth bared, ready to bite. Nerra recognized it as similar to the twisted shapes of the transformed back on the Isle of Hope, but this one seemed more animal somehow, as if it had started off as something that wasn't human.

There was no time to work out what, though, because it was already lunging at her. Ordinarily, Nerra would have run, wouldn't have known what else to do, but now instinct made her slash out with clawed hands, those claws slashing a gouge across the creature's flesh and forcing it to leap back. It stared at her, hissing and baring its teeth as if it might leap at Nerra again, and in that moment, two more joined it.

Nerra knew, in the same instinctive way that she knew the way the dragon soared, that while it would be easy enough to handle one of the lizard kin, three at once would be more difficult. They spread out around her, and Nerra suspected that she was going to die.

She saw the dragon plummet like a stone toward the earth, wings pinned back to its side, as it swooped in, dropping until it was almost at ground level before it opened its wings and beat them strongly, creating such a rush of air that Nerra found herself knocked from her feet. The lizard things were also sent sprawling.

The dragon opened its mouth, and somehow this time it wasn't fire that came out but a flickering, shadowy facsimile of it, which washed over the creatures without damaging the trees behind them. They cried out in pain and fell back, rushing into the forest.

Mine.

The word seemed to echo out over the forest, and it took Nerra a second to realize that it had nothing to do with anything vocal. Instead, the word seemed to echo in her mind, as if it were her brain translating something more primal into words that she could understand.

Nerra could only stare at the dragon now.

"You ... you're intelligent."

The dragon huffed, as if the very question were an insult. Gently, cautiously, Nerra reached out until she could touch its flank. It was warm and smooth, the power of the muscles beneath obvious as it shifted position slightly. Those great eyes stared down at Nerra, and she could feel everything the dragon was feeling in that moment: the curiosity, the sense of possessiveness. The dragon raised one claw, touching Nerra almost delicately, but even so, it drew blood.

She felt the connection that built in that moment, just a little, strengthening and joining, so that for an instant it felt as if she *was* the dragon. She saw herself as it saw her: something small and precious, changed into something as close to perfection as the human things of this world could be. She felt it scent the touch of her own dragon on her, and felt the moment when it extinguished that claim with a thought.

You are not the dragon Alith's. You belong to Shadr, the cooling of the flesh in the dark, first among the dragons.

"You're ..." Nerra struggled to understand. "You're their queen?"

The dragon seemed to consider it. *Yes, I am ... queen. And you are ... daughter of queen. You are to the Perfected as I am to my kind. I claim you, Nerra Queen's Daughter.*

"Claim?" Nerra said.

The Perfected are joined with us, bound as you will be. We created them to serve, and to move among the human things. One tried to claim you before, but it was too young.

Nerra found herself thinking of the blue of her dragon, but above her, the great black dragon blew a snort of flame.

You are mine, not hers. Soon, we will be bonded in truth.

Nerra didn't know how to react to that. A part of her told her that she ought to be terrified by the thought of anything, let alone a *dragon*, laying claim to her, but the other part of her, the one that bubbled beneath the surface, said that this was what she had been waiting for all her life. This was the reason she had been made into what she was, why she had suffered through so much in her life. This was the moment that made sense of all the rest of it.

Come.

The dragon, Shadr, lowered her neck, and it seemed obvious that she wanted Nerra to climb aboard her back. Nerra hesitated , some note of fear holding her back.

You do not need to fear me. You do not need to fear anything again.

Nerra felt the truth of that. She felt the power of the creature in front of her, the connection to the magic around them. While she was with Shadr, nothing could hurt her. Nothing could treat her differently because of the so-called disease affecting her. It hadn't been a disease; it had been making her what she always needed to be. She didn't understand all of it yet, but she didn't need to. She started to climb onto the dragon's back.

The scales above Shadr's neck were proud of the rest of her skin, providing enough grip that Nerra could cling to them as the dragon spread her wings and leapt into the sky, the fury of her wingbeats propelling them both up, and up. Nerra saw the ground below spread out like a map, the continent of Sarras becoming black stone and green jungle below, volcanos spread out in the distance, one of the largest growing closer with such rapidity that Nerra could barely believe that even the dragon could move so quickly.

As they grew closer, Nerra could see something on the slopes that seemed impossible: structures standing there that seemed as though they had been worked into the side of the volcano itself, high sided and smooth, with many open spaces marked out by pillars that reminded Nerra of the temple where the fountain had stood. Among them figures moved, the light shining off scales. They were, Nerra realized in shock, like her.

Even that wasn't all of it, because around the rim of the volcano, dragons roosted, and flew, and expelled breath high into the air. Most shot flames, but others blew out lightning, or ice, or clouds of what seemed like acid. The creatures there seemed to come in all the colors of the rainbow, some dull, some shining bright enough to nearly blind her. All were huge, but none of them seemed as large as Shadr, or as fearsome, or as powerful.

"There are ... so many," Nerra breathed, and even though the whisper was ripped away by the wind, she knew that the dragon beneath her heard her.

They wait for us.

"Wait for us?" Nerra repeated. "Why?"

We ride ... to war.

CHAPTER TEN

Erin was running out of men. She still had a few with her, but more had fallen, and others had gone off through the city to try to keep different pockets of the enemy at bay, but now...there weren't enough of them. There just weren't enough.

Not when the Southern Kingdom's soldiers were free to go through the city as they wished. The moment the rivers fell, they came pouring in, and Erin knew what that meant, however much she might hate it.

"Scatter," she said to her remaining men.

"What?" one of them asked.

"Scatter. Get to safety. Get out of the city if you can. Maybe there will be a way to come back from this later, but for now, there's no way to hold."

Erin would have given anything not to say those words, despised the idea of having to admit defeat after all they'd done, all they'd sacrificed to try to defend Royalsport. She knew that she couldn't ask her men to keep fighting though, not now that the numbers of the enemy were truly overwhelming.

"Hide among the people if you can't get out," she said, trying to hide the way that her heart was breaking. "We'll...we'll find a way to undo this."

"And what will you do?" one of the few who remained asked. "Head for the castle?"

"My family are there," Erin said. She looked over to where the House of Weapons stood above the next district. "But first...I have to help a friend. Go, all of you. *Go.*"

They ran, scattering to the wind, but Erin didn't wait to see which way they went. She was too busy running, trying to make it to the House of

Weapons before the men she knew would be closing in on it. She sprinted through the streets, keeping to the back alleys so that she would be harder to spot, but not slowing.

When she came to the nearest of the streams, Erin plunged into the rapidly drying bed. She came up out of the other side, into the district where the House of Weapons lay. She headed for it, hoping she would get there while there was still enough time to help Odd.

She found him through the sounds of violence coming from one of the side streets. The clash of blades could have been anyone, but instinct made Erin cut left between two buildings, toward the sound.

She saw Odd at the heart of a group of soldiers, running and then stopping, turning to kill one and then moving again. There were too many soldiers though, even for his skills.

Erin didn't hesitate. She plunged into the heart of them, striking out with her spear before she could even consider the fact that she should be afraid with so many soldiers there. She drove the point into a man's throat, struck another back with the haft of the spear, and forced her way forward.

A sword came at Erin and she deflected it more on instinct than with any conscious thought. By this point, she had been fighting for so long that she had no energy left to think about the way she was fighting, or the techniques involved, or anything but the flow of the battle. Erin struck back, bringing the man down, while Odd moved to her side, cutting down one man then another.

For an instant, a space opened up in the melee, and Erin pointed. "That way."

Odd nodded and kicked a man back out of the way. Erin paused a moment to slice the head of her spear across a soldier's throat, and then it was time for them both to run, sprinting breathlessly away, down a narrow alley with a wall at the end.

Erin scrambled up and over it, with Odd just a fraction of a second behind. Ahead, Erin could see a stack of crates and boxes set behind an inn, and when she got to them, she waited for Odd to pass, then jammed her spear into them, using it like a lever to overturn them, using the scatter of them to block the alley as they tumbled. She saw the few men who had made it over the wall stopping short at the tumble, only one of them managing to get through. She saw Odd kill him with a single sweeping cut.

Then they were running again, fueled by the fear of what would happen if they stopped, not halting until they had left the soldiers far behind.

Odd wasn't dead, and the sheer surprise of that filled him as he ran with Erin, only stopping when they reached the temporary shelter of a street stall that had been abandoned with the invasion. Odd leaned against it, catching his breath.

"You came back for me," he said, his surprise only growing.

Erin frowned. "Of course I came back for you."

She made it sound so obvious, yet Odd wasn't sure anyone else would have. He doubted they would have thought he was worth it.

"The House of Weapons has fallen," he said. "Swordmaster Wendros and I held out for a while, but there were too many of them."

Odd hated admitting his failure, especially to Erin.

"Wendros was there?" Erin said. "He…he was the one who taught me to use the spear instead of a sword."

Odd put a sympathetic hand on her shoulder. "I'm sorry, he didn't make it out of there."

He caught the flicker of pain across her features. She buried it as she seemed to bury so many other things, in anger.

"I'll kill them for that," Erin said.

"And I'll help you," Odd replied. "But for now, we need a plan."

"There are too many of them to fight openly," Erin said.

Odd could only agree with that. Even when Ravin's forces had been divided by the rush of the rivers, there had been too many of them. Now that they could all work together, they might as well try to hold back a storm.

"Then what?" he asked.

"I need…I need to get back to my sister," Erin said. That had been what Odd expected her to say. Erin was not one to run, or to put her own safety before that of others. "You don't have to come, though. You could hide in the city, sneak out when it's safe."

"I am *sworn* to your sister," Odd said, and anger seeped into those words whether he wanted it to or not. "I have done so much in my life, broken so many vows ... but I'll keep *this* one."

"I'm glad," Erin said, holding out her hand. Odd saw her glance toward the castle. There were men between them and it now, on the streets of the district they were in, and slowly pouring into the noble district. "Do you think we can get there without being seen?"

"No," Odd said. With so many men there, there was no way to do this quietly. A more sensible man might have tried anyway, and he would have died for it, bogged down in too many foes to fight. Which just left the *other* option. A trace of the old madness took the place of his anger, and Odd gave Erin a wild grin. "Race you there."

He set off running, because there was no point in hiding when soon the city's streets would be filled with soldiers. Better to run, better to eat up the distance before anyone could begin to imagine that they would do something like this.

Erin ran with him, and Odd laughed, because when all hope was lost, what else was there to do *but* embrace the wild joy of it all. A soldier stepped into Odd's path, and he didn't even slow as he cut the man down.

"Keep running!" he shouted to Erin as they raced over a riverbed, up into the noble district. He could make out the castle walls ahead, gray and imposing, solid looking to anyone who didn't know about war. Another soldier tried to move in front of Odd, and the former knight cut him down just as swiftly as the first.

More men came, and Odd saw Erin pause as she thrust her spear through one, another two moving in to try to attack her. Odd turned and cut one down, then grabbed Erin's hand, pulling her on.

"We don't stop," he said to her. "Not for that, not for—"

His foot caught on a loose cobble and he fell. Men were coming at him even as he came up, and Odd barely parried the first attack sent his way. A blade scraped across his side, and he winced in pain as he killed the man who wielded it. Erin was there then, lancing her spear through another man's throat, making a gap, letting them run again.

They kept running, kept killing, and the walls of the castle grew closer. Erin was swift, and it was all Odd could do to keep up with her. There was a problem though, because the gates of the castle were firmly shut, and with Ravin's forces closing in, there was no way that they would open for them.

Then Odd saw figures standing on top of the walls, and it was clear that one of the guards there recognized them, because he was waving. Odd saw the thin line of a rope drop from the wall, and he raced for it.

Erin got there first and started to haul herself up, climbing the rope hand over hand with her spear strapped to her back. Odd followed, and shouting below said that their climb was not going unnoticed. Arrows clattered from the walls around them. Worse, Odd felt the tension on the rope change and looked down to see men climbing below him, following after either to kill him or take the walls.

Odd thought for a moment, wrapped the rope tightly about one arm, and drew a knife with the other hand.

It seemed to take forever to slice through the rope. Forever in which the men below him were still climbing, close enough that one was able to reach out for him even as the last strands gave way. Odd felt a hand clamp to his foot while below him, the others on the line fell to their deaths. Odd stared down at the face of the man there, saw the fear, saw the anger. Then he stamped down once, twice, hard enough that the man let go in a rush, falling with a scream.

Odd resumed climbing, and as he reached the top, he was surprised to see that it wasn't just Erin there. Lenore was there too, helping him over, pulling him within the safety of the walls.

"I knew you'd both come back," she said. "I'm glad you're safe."

Odd sighed with relief, even though he knew right then that none of them were safe.

"My mother is in the keep's great hall," Lenore said. "We should join her. It will be safer there than here."

"I don't think anywhere is going to be safe for long," Erin said. "But we're probably better off there than here."

As if in answer to those words, Odd heard Ravin's men starting to hammer on the gates, trying to break through. Odd knew that as soon as they decided to stop trying to break through and just climbed, this would be done. At least, for now, they had a little time.

They ran for the keep, while behind him, Odd could already hear the metal on stone clink of the first grapnels being thrown.

CHAPTER ELEVEN

Devin trekked on horseback down through the far north of the kingdom, with the wolf-like form of Sigil by his side and the need to be home pushing him onward. The wind whipped at his dark hair, while the leanness of his body wrapped in chain mail and leathers was probably the only human form to be seen for leagues on either side.

The cold bit at him, even though the snow had stopped falling once he was down off the slopes of the hills. Beside him, Sigil seemed untroubled by it, deep gray fur clearly protecting him from the weather, the strange, darker patch in the shape of some mystical rune standing out against the rest of it.

The landscape around Devin was wild and empty. Trees stood here and there, but they mostly stood alone. Grass and moss clung to stones, but there was little farmland this far north. There were still villages here and there, but even so, Devin couldn't remember the last time he had spoken to another human.

No, that wasn't true. He had spoken to Sir Twell before the Knight of the Spur had frozen to death under the weight of a would-be mage's assault on the mountain. He had spoken to that mage before he had dragged a fragment of the unfinished sword through the man's flesh to bring him down for what he'd done.

Thoughts of the knight inevitably brought with them thoughts of how difficult this journey had been, traveling the kingdom to try to find the fragments of the sword. There had been dangers at each step, and Devin had lost friends along the way. Sir Twell had died here in the far north, while Sir Halfin the Swift had been brought down by a treelike monster fueled by the magic of one of the shards.

Devin pressed on for a while longer before he stopped in the shadow of a single marker stone, long grown over with moss until it seemed almost like a natural part of the landscape. Devin went around it until he found a spot under it that was in the lee of the wind. It didn't feel warm there, exactly, but at least it didn't have the same crushing cold as before. He tethered his horse in place, feeding it grain from one of its saddlebags. With only one horse left now, there was plenty.

He drew sticks together, then took out a flint and steel to start a fire. Devin paused, staring at his hand. He could still remember the feeling of stopping the storm, what it had been like to balance all the forces that had been involved in it and apply power in just the right place to bring it to a halt. If he could do *that* with magic, couldn't he do this?

Devin considered the sticks that he'd gathered, tried to focus on them while Sigil sat to the side, regarding him with a level gaze that seemed to have more intelligence in it than a wolf should have. Devin tried to reach out for them, tried to coax flames from them. Nothing happened.

"How can I stop a *storm* and not do this?" Devin asked Sigil.

The creature moved over to him and Devin reached out. His fingers brushed the spot where the rune symbol lay on the creature's fur. As he did so, Devin felt something shift inside him, and now he could feel the magic in the air around him. He reached out through it, and now he could feel the sticks that he'd put in place, feel all the potential that lay within them. He concentrated on that potential, focusing in on one spot, tighter and tighter. Then he pushed magic into it. It felt similar to the way he might have blown on an ember to coax it into flame, but it was magic that he blew its way, not breath.

It was hard, far harder than he had ever thought it might be, but as Devin poured in magic, he saw the faint glow of an ember within the cage of sticks that formed his fire. It was small, glowing red, then orange, brightening even as Devin watched. It caught and grew, turning into something more, expanding little by little, until finally a fire burned in front of him.

"Well done, you have started to learn."

Devin started at the sound of Master Grey's voice, and looked up to see the sorcerer sitting across from him, on the opposite side of the fire. Except there was something wrong about the way he looked. The white robes and bald skull were the same, the hawk-like features unchanged, but the whole seemed to flicker slightly in the light of the fire, distorting each time the flames shifted.

"You're not really here, are you?" Devin asked.

"This is...think of it as a waking dream. A projection of my being," Master Grey said. "You can see it, because your mind is close enough to the state required. Tell me, what do you think of the magic you have just done?"

"I think it would have been easier to use the flint and steel to start a fire," Devin said.

To his surprise, he saw Master Grey nod.

"That is one of the lessons of magic that is hardest to learn. It can do great things, but it is still subject to rules and limits. We cannot just wish things into happening; the power for it must come from somewhere. For those who work carefully, it is about balancing the threads of things until we find a way to make them happen as we wish. Others take shortcuts, and draw power from darker places."

Devin wasn't sure if the fire flickered again then, or if he saw Master Grey shudder.

"I calmed a storm," he said. "I...felt the way it worked, and I *knew* where to push it to change it."

Master Grey smiled at that. "That is magic at its purest. People think of spells, but in truth, most so-called spells are ways to draw the mind to what it should understand to change things."

The sheer enormity of that struck Devin in a rush.

"So I can change the world?" Devin asked. "I can do anything?"

Master Grey's smile turned into a laugh. "You start one fire and you think you can reshape the world. The truth is more complex. Every time you use magic, you will have to see the way things fit together, and every time, it will be different. Some days, it will come as easy as breathing, and others, you won't be able to see it at all. Some things you will have a talent for, and others you will never grasp. You have a natural instinct for star metal, but the rest...you will need to keep working, Devin."

That sounded no clearer than anything else Master Grey said, as if the whole business of magic was not something to be learned once, but rather, learned over and over again each time a spell needed to be cast. Devin tried to grasp that, but it seemed like too much. Instead, he focused on the mention of star metal, and took out the pouch where he'd stowed the fragments of the sword.

"I found the pieces of the unfinished sword," Devin said. "When I get back to Royalsport, I can—"

"Do not come back," Master Grey said, and those words made Devin's eyes widen.

"What? Why not?" Devin asked.

"Royalsport is not the place where the sword must be forged," Master Grey said. "It must be forged here, in the wild places. *This* is where you will find the strength to do it."

"But I..." How could Devin explain that he wanted to get back to Royalsport more than anything? That he wanted to see the city again? That he wanted to see Lenore so much that it hurt? Every step Devin had taken on this trip had been fueled by the thought that once it was done he might be able to go back to her, see her again.

"It *must* be here," Master Grey said, although he didn't seem to want to provide more of an explanation than that. Even as it was, the few cryptic things he'd said probably counted as the most he'd explained about magic in all the time Devin had known him. "You must begin the work, and in that, you'll have help."

Devin caught his glance across to the spot where Sigil sat, watching the conversation almost as if the creature could take in every word of it.

"You know what he is?" Devin asked. No normal wolf had a symbol like that in its fur, or followed a man so closely.

"A creature more connected to magic than most," Master Grey said. "You might find him a valuable conduit in the days to come."

"What *is* coming?" Devin asked.

"Focus on finishing the sword," Master Grey said. "That must be done, or so much of this will be for nothing. Craft your forge, use your magic. Ready the blade for the time when it must be used."

"But *when* is that?" Devin shot back. He was sick of never getting real answers from Master Grey; of him talking as if everything Devin was going to do was laid out ahead of him, but never letting Devin see any of it.

"I can stay no longer," Master Grey said. "Recent events have taxed my strength. You have all the tools you need, Devin."

"What recent events?" Devin asked, but the sorcerer's image was already fading, the flickering of the fire starting to take over from it. "What's happening?"

"Finish the sword." Master Grey's voice seemed to come from a distance now, and there was no sign of him left. "That's all that matters. Finish the sword, Devin."

CHAPTER TWELVE

Aethe sighed with relief as she saw her daughters arrive in the great hall of the castle's keep, Lenore escorted by Erin and that strange monk/ knight who spent so much time with her now. She had a brief moment to feel happy that her daughters were safe before she realized the stupidity of that: none of them were safe here.

She felt old in that moment. She was sure she *looked* old too, grief at her husband's death and fear of what might happen next adding lines to her face, gray to her hair. There was no time at a moment like this to spend on making sure she looked perfect.

There should have been no time to go over and hug her daughters yet, either, when there were enemies battering at their gates, but Aethe took a moment to do it anyway, moving to Erin and Lenore, then pulling them close to her.

"I'm so glad you're back here," she said to Erin. "You're wounded!"

"It's not that bad," Erin said.

"When I heard you'd gone out into the city, I thought you were lost."

"Your daughter fights too well for that," the monk beside her daughters said. "She saved my life out there."

"And Odd has saved mine before," Erin insisted. She squirmed back from Aethe. Some things couldn't be changed in a matter of moments. She couldn't mend things that had taken a lifetime to fall apart.

"How bad is it out there?" Aethe asked.

"Bad," Erin said. "The men I took with me are gone, either dead or hiding. The sorcerer..."

"I know," Aethe said. "I sent a man to find him, but he's gone."

The monk with her daughter coughed. "With respect, your majesty, the location of Master Grey is not what matters now. What matters is that men are trying to breach the walls as we speak."

"And we have too few men to hold them there," Aethe said. She caught the former Sir Oderick's expression. "I do know *something* of these things, sir knight."

"I am a knight no longer, your majesty."

"As I am currently no queen," Aethe said. She turned to the nearest of her retainers. "Pull men back to the inner keep," she commanded. "They can try a volley or two if they can manage it safely, but then I want them back here. The walls will hold them for a moment, but we cannot stand there. Here, the doors are iron, and with a smaller space to defend, we have more chance to hold it. We can keep them out as long as we need."

She did not say the obvious: that no keep could hold out an army forever. Still, this one had its own wells, and enough stores that those within might last months before starvation forced an end to things. In that time, they might find a way to bring help to Royalsport. At the very least, they might force Ravin to negotiate as his siege stalled, and that might be enough to keep the people Aethe cared about safe.

"Go get yourselves patched up," Aethe said to Erin and Odd. "Lenore, go with them. They will keep you safe, no matter what happens." She turned to the others in the hall. "The enemy is attacking our walls. They will hold them for a time, but this is the time when we must stand together."

"And where is the king?" one of the nobles demanded. "Where is he, at this time of crisis?"

This was the moment that Aethe had been waiting for. She started to gesture for a man of the House of Scholars to step forward, a man so old that it was a wonder to Aethe that he was still standing there in his black robes and chains of knowledge depicting fields in which he had proven his expertise beyond all others. The one that mattered was the iron chain of the law.

She was about to let him make his pronouncement when a servant ran forward.

"Your majesty," the girl said, and Aethe opened her mouth to reprimand her for speaking at this of all moments. "Your majesty, they've caught the boy who killed the king."

Instantly, Aethe felt the blood draining from her face. In that moment, none of it mattered. They could bring down the castle and kill everyone there; in that moment, all she cared about was seeing the face of the boy who had killed her husband.

"Bring him here," she said, keeping a tight rein on the fury in her words. Guards came into the great hall, dragging, practically carrying, a small form between them.

The boy was small, perhaps ten or eleven years old, dressed in dirt stained page's clothes, his sandy blond hair just as streaked with filth. *This* was who had killed her husband?

Aethe held out her hand to a guard. "Pass me your sword."

"Your majesty?"

"Now!"

The man did as she commanded, and Aethe stepped toward the boy, blade raised, ready to plunge it through his heart. The boy cried out, trying to squirm free.

It was at that moment that Aethe saw his left hand. It was smaller even than the rest of him, withered and crippled, made into a kind of claw that could clearly never be used to hold anything. Yet the wound that had killed her husband had been that of a large dagger; large enough that a boy this small would have had to hold it in two hands.

For a moment, Aethe's anger almost overruled her sense, demanding that she drive the blade home anyway, but she held back. She forced herself to think, to focus on the details that seemed so wrong. How did she know that this boy had killed Godwin? Because Vars said so. Did she trust her stepson so much that she would disregard the evidence in *this*?

Why would Vars lie? No, that wasn't the question. There were all kinds of reasons Vars would lie; he lied almost as often as he spoke. Yet why would he lie about *this*, with his father dead?

"Tell me," Aethe said. "Tell me what happened."

"I..." The boy was white as a ghost and shaking. The guards still clung to his arms as if they feared he might kill her as he had the king.

"No," Aethe said, lowering her blade, "let him go."

The guards loosened their grip on the squirming boy.

"What happened?" Aethe said more gently. "They say that you killed the king."

"I didn't!" the boy exclaimed. "I promise!"

"I believe you," Aethe said, with a look toward the hand that could never have held the knife. "What's your name?"

"M-Merin, your majesty."

"Well, Merin," Aethe said. "Why would Vars say that you killed King Godwin?"

"I..." The boy looked more frightened than ever. "I didn't do it."

"I know," Aethe said.

"I didn't do it; he did!"

Those words caught Aethe off guard, shock hitting her even as every other instinct told her that she shouldn't *be* shocked. She didn't want to believe that even Vars could be capable of something like that, yet the moment she heard it, Aethe knew it was the truth.

"Tell me," Aethe said, reaching out to lay a hand on the boy's shoulder. "Tell me what he did."

"He said I was to look after the king," Merin said. "And then I heard him shouting, him and the king. They were arguing, and I looked to see what was going on, and...and...I saw Prince Vars stab him. I saw it. He *chased* me. He tried to kill me too!"

Again, a part of Aethe didn't want to believe it, even while the rest of her recognized the truth when she heard it. It was *exactly* the kind of thing Vars might do, even though she wanted to believe that no one would. He'd done it.

He'd killed her husband.

Anger and grief, rage and pain roared through Aethe, and she roared with it, crying out her anguish so that all the others present in the great hall stared at her. She pointed a single, shaking finger at the law master from the House of Scholars.

"Say it," she said. *"Say it!"*

The man stood before the assembled crowd of nobles, caught a little unawares by the weight of the gazes that fell on him. Even so, the sternness of Aethe's expression was greater, and he started to speak.

"In the ancient laws of our kingdom, it is stated by..." Aethe's gesture stopped him from stating all the places that it was stated in detail. "It is *stated* that in any situation where a king is no longer fit to rule, another can rule in his stead. A regent can be appointed, as Vars was to his father, but there are older laws that he did not know of. It is possible... it is possible to go further. The nobles of the land can declare... can declare a new ruler."

"In *any* situation," Aethe said, her voice carrying above the sudden noise of the hall. "I was going to come to you with this because my husband's son has fled, and I thought his cowardice was enough. I was going to come to you because you are the nobles of the kingdom, and we need a real ruler right now. Now... does *anyone* here believe that Vars is fit to rule? Does anyone want to take his place instead of me, when we have the defense of this keep to organize, when all of our lives may be on the line?"

Aethe looked around them, and the nobles were silent for so long that for a moment or two she truly thought that they might pick another, or that they might be so beholden to Vars that they might go along with him even now.

Then one of them called out the words Aethe had longed to hear. "All hail Queen Aethe!"

Other voices joined them, one by one, rising to a crescendo. "All hail Queen Aethe! All hail Queen Aethe!"

"Good. Now, get back to reinforcing this keep!" Aethe ordered. "I want it impenetrable by the time the enemy get to it!"

CHAPTER THIRTEEN

Vars was discovering that there were many different kinds of fear. There was the sharp terror that had come when King Ravin's soldiers were standing over him. There was the dull fear as they hauled him through the city, cut through with irritation that these men would *dare* to lay hands upon a king.

Now, as the men dragged him into the space before the castle, he felt a whole new collection of fears. There was fear of the sheer awesome violence of the army that battered at the gates, men throwing grappling hooks to try to scale the walls and working to break down the doors that blocked their way. There was fear of being dragged into that violence, because men were firing back down at the attackers, sending down a volley of arrows that barely seemed to do anything to their numbers.

The greatest wash of fear, though, came when the men brought Vars to the figure who stood at the heart of it all, directing the attack. He was broad and muscled in gilded armor, a great sword by his side, a crown of platinum sitting atop close-cropped dark hair. A tightly curling beard fell down to his chest, while dark eyes stared at him without a hint of pity or kindness. Those eyes filled Vars with more terror than all the rest of it put together.

"What have you brought me?" he asked the guards with Vars. Above them, men were starting to mount the walls, the defenders fleeing. Vars heard screams and the sounds of battle from those who weren't quick enough.

"My king..." one of the men said. "This man claims...he claims that he is the king of this place."

Ravin started to laugh, his voice deep and booming. Then he stopped, staring at Vars. Vars could almost imagine him taking in the details of Vars's noble clothes, the small things that marked him out as who he was. As he did that, the steady hammering of axes against the gates seemed to mirror the frantic beating of Vars's heart.

"Tell me truly," he said, staring at Vars. "Who are you? Remember, there are those among my Quiet Men who will have been close enough to you to touch you. They will know who you are."

"I am King Vars of the Northern Kingdom," Vars said, trying to summon whatever courage he could. He wished that it were more.

King Ravin stared at him, and it seemed to Vars almost as if the man could see right through to the heart of him.

"Yes," he said. "I believe you. And of course, if I find out that you're lying, I will have you flayed alive."

The calm way in which he said that was almost worse than if he'd raised his voice. Somehow, even that calmness floated over the sounds of the fighting. It was the kind of authority that Vars could never have managed. King Ravin lifted his sword, holding it lightly in two hands as if testing the weight of it.

"This sword is called Heartsplitter," he said. "I have used it to kill more men than you can count. I used it to bring together a nation at war with itself and forge a strong Southern Kingdom. I will use it today to take the throne that should always have been mine by right, along with the rest." He lifted it to Vars's throat. "Tell me, 'King' Vars, why should I not use it to cut you down?"

"Because..." Vars tried to be brave, tried to hold onto some scrap of respect, some semblance that he wasn't a coward. With the weight of Ravin's sword resting at his throat, though, even that was quickly ebbing away. "I can help you. I can bring all of this to an end."

King Ravin cocked his head to one side. From somewhere behind them, Vars heard the sound of the castle gates splintering open. "We will see. Follow."

King Ravin stalked off ahead of Vars, and for a moment, Vars had a clear view of his back. He knew that, if he had been someone braver, like his father, he could have taken that moment to grab a weapon and drive it into King Ravin, to end him once and for all.

That, though, would have meant death. He was surrounded by Ravin's army, and would be cut down in a matter of seconds once he did it. His brother might have done it, although he'd have been more likely to challenge Ravin to some heroic duel, but then, Rodry had always been an idiot. Vars had no interest in forging some glorious legacy as the sacrifice needed to save the kingdom. He wanted to be *alive* at the end of this.

That meant that he followed King Ravin as the Northern Kingdom's ruler made his way to the open gate. Vars heard screams as they approached, and they were more horrible than anything Vars had heard before. The doors hung like the ragged remnants of a cloak now, moving in the wind.

There were bodies in the space beneath the gatehouse, in the armor of King Ravin's forces. They lay trapped up against a portcullis, horrific burns covering them.

"It is common to drop oil, or sand," King Ravin said. "I was going to go over the wall, but let's see how much they value their king."

He shoved Vars forward into the space below the gatehouse, and Vars stared up at the arrow slits there.

"Wait!" Vars screamed out. "Don't kill me! I am Vars! I am your king!"

Behind him, King Ravin's booming laugh came again. "And now we know how readily you will betray them. Do you think that the men who went over the walls haven't taken the gatehouse by now? Raise the portcullis!"

He called that out as an order to unseen soldiers beyond the gate, and a second later, the portcullis started to rise. King Ravin strode past Vars into the courtyard of the castle, and Vars had to follow because the soldiers who came after him gave him no choice.

There were bodies scattered around that space, of soldiers and servants cut down by Ravin's men. There were almost none of the Southern Kingdom's soldiers dead among them, their numbers too overwhelming for the defenders even to start to fight back.

Ravin strode over to where the castle's keep stood, his men hammering at the door, but seeming to make no impact. Arrows came down from the windows, bringing down the soldiers who assaulted it.

"The keep is stronger than the rest," Ravin said next to Vars. "They have enough defenders to hold it, even as they cannot hold the outer walls. It is time for you to do your part."

"What…what do you want me to do?" Vars said, as if that mattered. As if he wouldn't do *anything* if he thought it would help to save his life.

"You are their king, aren't you?" Ravin shot back. "Command them to surrender."

Vars stared up at the keep, stood there with his arms outstretched, hoping that they would see him. His fear told him all the things that might happen if he failed.

"Listen to me!" he called out to the emptiness of the windows. "See me! I am King Vars, *your* king!"

Even he could hear the desperation in his voice as he said it. Why couldn't he manage a true tone of command? The falling arrows stopped for a moment or two, and Vars thought he could see glimpses of faces in the windows. Was that Aethe there above in one of the highest? She seemed to be staring down at Vars with something…something that looked a lot like hatred.

"The city is lost," Vars called out. "The *kingdom* is lost. I have spoken with King Ravin, and I believe him to be a fair man. Our only hope is to negotiate a surrender. Open the doors to the keep."

No one moved. Certainly, the doors didn't open.

"Open the doors!" Vars insisted. "I demand it as your king!"

"You are not our king," Aethe called from above. "Not any longer. Not after you murdered my husband. Archers, kill him!"

Vars jumped back as arrows fell around him, clattering off the cobbles of the courtyard. He turned to run and King Ravin caught him one-handed, holding him in place the way another man might have held a child, or a dog.

"It seems you are no use to me after all," he said. "I would threaten to kill you if they did not open their keep, but I suspect they would only beg me to do it. Take him away," he said to his guards. "Kill him slowly."

This terror was worse than all the others, seeming to come out of the depths of Vars's soul. It was, he realized, who he was—a coward to his core.

"Wait! Wait, I can still get you inside," he said. "Just let me live, and I can show you a passage to the inside. I can still help."

King Ravin stared at him, and for a moment, Vars thought that he might kill him anyway. Then the Southern Kingdom's ruler lowered his blade.

"Very well. Show my men this way inside. If it works, I will do *more* than let you live. I will let you continue to be a king."

Vars swallowed, hating himself for what he was about to do, hating the coward that he was, and how easily he could betray all those he knew. Even so, he felt relief flooding through him, almost overwhelming.

"That's..."

"And if you fail again, in even the smallest way, you will wish that I had killed you when I first saw you."

CHAPTER FOURTEEN

For most of the next hour, Aethe seethed in anger that the arrows her archers fired had missed Vars. She wanted to shout out in rage at that, wanted to scream her frustration to the heavens. She wanted to go down there, throw open the doors, and strangle him with his bare hands.

There was no time for that though, because they still had to organize the defense of the keep. It *should* be impenetrable, at least for now. The doors were thick iron, and the walls were thicker stone, while the space was small enough that the weight of an army didn't matter as much. Only a few could attack at any time. Still, Aethe knew that the heart of the people within mattered as well.

That was why she was touring the keep, trying to make sure that all was in order. She came to another group of archers, who seemed to be taking pot shots at any of Ravin's soldiers who came close.

"Don't waste your arrows," she told them. "Focus on any who make actual attempts on the doors. Ravin is cunning and callous enough to send men to draw our arrows until we run out."

She kept going through the keep. It was better if she kept busy. It would draw her mind from the hatred she felt for Vars, and the need to see justice for Godwin's killer. So she stalked the halls, trying to organize, trying to make sure that those within were prepared.

"Do all who want weapons have them?" she asked a servant.

"Well, the soldiers, your majesty, but—"

"If they find a way into the keep, do you think they will only kill soldiers?" Aethe asked. "Anyone who can hold a weapon is to be armed. Those who do not know how to use one are to be shown. Ask my daughter. Erin and this … Sir Odd are probably the best we have at the moment for the task."

"Yes, your majesty."

The man hurried away, but already another was coming to her. "I have been organizing an inventory of the keep's food supplies," he said. "Several nobles have been helping themselves to the wine and the food."

"I will speak to them," Aethe said. She stopped herself. "No, I will *command* them. Let it be known that, at a time like this, any who take more than their share are stealing from the rest of us, and making it more likely that the keep will fall. If any more take what is not theirs, they will be treated like the thieves they are, and hanged."

"Yes, your majesty."

One after another, they came to her, because making herself the queen meant that she had made herself the one they looked to for answers on everything. Where should they place barricades? Which guards should go where? What should happen when two nobles who were at odds with one another were forced into the same close confines? It reminded Aethe a little of what it had been like when she'd been a mother to small children, and she smiled at the thought of her daughters running around, playing and arguing, Lenore complaining that Erin had climbed some dangerously high tree, Nerra needing to be kept from the sight of the world because of her sickness...

Aethe was still caught in her daydream of better times when the boy Merin came up to her, accompanied by a servant.

"You have something to say to me, Merin?" she asked. The boy was looking nervous, but that was understandable after all he had been through.

"They say...they say you're trying to make the castle impossible to get into," the boy said.

"That's right," Aethe replied.

"You...you've blocked the way out, then?" he asked. "The one I used when...when Prince Vars was chasing me?"

Fear filled Aethe in an instant. "What way out? Show me. Show me at once!"

She hurried along the keep's corridors, following the boy as he led the way. She was still only halfway there when she heard the screams.

Instinct made her run toward them, sprinting down the stairs of the keep toward what was now the sound of violence: the scrape of steel and the angry bellowing of fighting men, the screams of those who were wounded or dying or scared and the thud of footsteps against stone.

Aethe rounded a corner and found herself staring at a battle, with soldiers in the red and purple of King Ravin's forces pouring into a small hallway through a doorway she hadn't even known existed. It took her only a moment to think of how they might have found out about this route into the castle.

Vars.

Her hatred flared again as the soldiers pushed their way into the hall. They hacked at all who stood around them, whether it was soldiers trying to fight them, or servants trying to get away, or anyone else.

The few guards there fought bravely in the enclosed space, and Aethe saw them kill soldier after soldier who came at them. One cut a man down, parried another blow, and set himself in the middle of the hallway. He struck down another foe, hacked at a third...

Then a soldier with a spear plunged it through his chest.

More surged forward, and Aethe could see that their numbers were simply too great. She saw one of her guards cut down, then another, because no matter how bravely they fought, it wasn't enough. She saw them pushed back by the sheer weight of numbers, unable to keep up with the press of their foes. She saw a man hacked down by an axe, a servant brought down almost by accident by the sweep of a sword.

She was almost grateful that she couldn't see Erin there in the violence of it all. It was the kind of fight that her daughter might have thrown herself into headfirst, and the thought of that terrified Aethe, because she couldn't imagine anyone surviving in the chaos of that melee.

She knew this wouldn't hold for long. "Back!" she called out. "Back to the great hall!"

She ran for the great hall with the others, a glance back telling her that a small number of the guards continued to fight, holding the onrushing soldiers long enough to give them a chance. Aethe felt a twinge of pain at their sacrifice, but also gratitude for the time they were buying for her and the others to escape.

She ran for the great hall, and saw people streaming into it, servants and soldiers, nobles and their retainers. All those who could get there were pouring in, struggling to the last place that seemed as though it might be safe.

Aethe was one of the last in. She looked around and couldn't see her daughters. Were they in some other part of the keep? Were they safer like that, or in more danger? There was no way to know, and that was the worst part of all, even as the guards shut the doors, barring them and hoping.

While the others chattered amongst themselves, seeking reassurance, Aethe waited for the hammering to start on those doors. She stood there and tried to school her face so that it wouldn't show any of the fear that she felt as she stared at those doors and saw how weak they were, how fragile. They were barred, but the bar was nowhere near thick enough to hold back an army.

It would fall, and then…then there would be a slaughter. So Aethe waited, and knew that what she was waiting for was her death.

Instead of hammering or the thud of axes, though, the only thing that came was the simple rapping of a hand against the wood.

That rapping was enough to stop all the chatter around Aethe. The great hall went still and silent, that sound feeling like a portent of doom, announcing death. A voice followed, deep and sure, powerful and deadly.

"I am Ravin, King of the Three Kingdoms," the voice said. "You have lost. Your castle has fallen, and now so has your keep."

"What do you want?" Aethe replied.

"Ah, Queen Aethe. It is time for you to open this door."

"And then you slaughter us all?" Aethe asked.

"I could do that in a heartbeat," Ravin replied, through the oak of the door. "I could have my men batter this door down and then kill every person they find. I could do this, and I will, if you don't give me what I want."

"And what is that?" Aethe repeated. Behind her, she could practically feel the fear of the others in the hall. Just a glance showed them staring at her, hoping, as if she might have some way to save them from this.

"I want you to acknowledge that I rule here. You will open this door, and you will submit to me. Do that, and you will live, at least for now. Fail to do that, and I will kill every person I find in this place."

Aethe hesitated, trying to think of something that she could say, some option that she had that might help with this. There was nothing though, only the bleak, empty feeling that everything they had tried had failed.

"I will count to three," Ravin said beyond the door. "One ..."

Aethe looked around the hall. The people were looking to each other, looking to her, almost frantically.

"Two ..."

"We surrender," Aethe said, calling it out loudly enough to carry beyond the door. "We surrender."

She went to the door and unbarred it herself. It swung open under the lightest of touches, revealing King Ravin there with his men. Those men poured into the great hall, surrounding the others there. King Ravin locked eyes with Aethe for a second and she could feel the satisfaction there, the triumph.

"Follow," he said.

He strode past her, heading for the spot where the throne stood. As his guards hemmed her in, Aethe had no choice but to follow, trailing in his wake as he went to the throne. Vars was there too, and Aethe shot him a look of hate, but he just looked away.

She had to watch as King Ravin went to the throne, had to watch as he stood before it, as he turned, as he set himself down on it, sword across his knees.

"From this moment," he said, "there is no Northern Kingdom and Southern Kingdom. There are no separate kings. I am Ravin, ruler of the Three Kingdoms. Do you acknowledge that, Aethe, wife of Godwin?"

Aethe had to swallow back bile to say the next words. "I do."

"Then kneel," he said. "Kneel before your king."

Aethe knelt. She let herself drop to the stones of the floor, bowing her head, but it wasn't in submission. It was simpler than that: she didn't want Ravin to see her face. She didn't want him to see the hate there, or the promise hiding behind her eyes.

It was a simple one: this wasn't done. She would find a way to turn this around, and find a way to kill him, no matter what it took.

CHAPTER FIFTEEN

Nerra clung to Shadr as the great black dragon circled down toward the buildings that dotted the side of the volcano. She landed among them with a rush of air moving in every direction, and the people who had been there scattered before her to clear a landing site.

Nerra stared at them, and at the settlement around them, in wonder. From the air, it had all seemed strange enough, but now buildings of smooth, almost melted stone surrounded her, rising up in towers and ziggurats. Carvings stood on the side of some, and those depicted dragons moving above the world, their breath searing out over it in fire, or lightning, or frost. There was a whole city's worth of it, some of the buildings standing only as overgrown ruins or marks on the ground, but a city, nonetheless. Nerra had never known that Sarras possessed such a thing.

The people...

"They're like me," Nerra breathed as she saw them moving through the city. At least, many of them were. Some wore clothes of elegant silk or woven cotton, while others seemed to move with just the resplendent beauty of iridescent scales. Those scales came in a multitude of colors, so that the deep blue of her own scales hardly seemed out of place.

Like you, but not like you, Shadr declared. *You are mine.*

Even so, as she dismounted, Nerra couldn't take her eyes from the others there. There were so many of them, more than she could have imagined. There were others too, who moved through the streets in the bestial forms of those who had been twisted by the dragon-sickness. She flinched as she heard one snarl like something animal, teeth bared.

She felt Shadr's amusement through the connection between them.

You do not need to fear the lesser. They are not what you are, could never be *what you are.*

"And what am I?" Nerra asked.

The dragon's great yellow eyes stared down at her. *You are Perfected.*

"Who *are* all these people?" Nerra asked. "I know they're like me, but who are they? Where do they come from?"

Again Nerra felt the dragon's amusement.

From everywhere human-things are found. Go, walk among them. Do you see the largest temple?

Nerra could see it: an open set of pillars clustered around a court-yard larger than most fields. The space within was constructed of concentric circles of stone, each of a different color, some of them shining like gems.

See this place. Meet me there. Shadr's wings beat, and in an instant, the dragon was taking to the air.

"Meet you there for what?" Nerra called after her.

To complete our joining.

Nerra stared as the dragon set off toward the broad circle of the temple, then started off after her, walking up through the city, along the side of the volcano.

It was a beautiful place of broad streets and flat-roofed buildings, towers with elegant perches built into the top and cleared spaces that it took Nerra a moment to realize the purpose of. They were for dragons to land. The whole city was designed with dragons in mind. This was *their* place, not a place for people as she knew them.

She walked through the city, watching it pass around her, and now that she knew the secret of it, it seemed that she saw more of it than she had before. She saw the way that decorations had been designed in more colors than any human eye could hope to see, the way that every space was open enough to allow for dragons to land, and even the towers were spaced out enough that they would not impede their flight.

Around Nerra, the scaled people of the place carried out all the business of a city anywhere. They talked and they laughed. They stopped at fountains, seemingly caught between the human impulse to meet others and the lizard-like one to bask in the sun. They sold food, or small things.

The lesser creatures, the ones who had not transformed as well or as fully as Nerra, moved among them, something between servants and pets. Nerra saw them carrying heavy crates and working on buildings under the command of those who were more like her. Several of them came up to her, sniffing at her, and a golden-scaled woman of her kind shooed them away.

"You must be firm with them," she said. She was taller than Nerra, and wore robes of simple white that brushed the ground, the golden tip of a tail sweeping out beyond it. "You are the new one; the one Shadr has chosen."

"How did you know that?" Nerra asked.

"Everyone knows," she replied. "My dragon told me. I am Irae, claimed by K'ta."

"It is good to meet you," Nerra said, holding out a hand. To her surprise, she found her claws extending.

"You will get used to it," Irae said with what Nerra assumed was a smile. It was hard to read her more reptilian features. "I remember how strange it was when I was first changed."

"It doesn't feel strange," Nerra said. "It feels *right.*"

"Ah," Irae said. "Perhaps you are truly suited this. Now, I should not keep you here. Your dragon is waiting."

Nerra nodded, grateful that she'd had the chance to meet at least one of the others like her. She set off again in the direction of the temple, up along the broad streets, weaving her way among the others.

The closer she got to the temple space, the more she was able to take in the sheer scale of it. The pillars around it were all bigger than she could have imagined, each on the scale of a house or a tower, each more than big enough to support the dragons that perched on some of them. Those stared down, some opening and closing great wings, some stretching and curling as they grew more comfortable. As Nerra stepped into the circle of pillars, more started to land, eyes staring down at her from every side.

Her eyes were on the spot at the heart of it all where Shadr sat, waiting. Nerra went to her, crossing over the circles of stone one after another. There was one of the humanoid figures like Nerra there, a male who stood and watched as Nerra approached.

Nerra felt the connection between her and Shadr come more alive as she grew closer.

Lie there, Shadr commanded her, indicating a spot with a claw. Nerra did so, staring up at the sky, trying to work out what was going to happen next. She saw Shadr's claws whip round, scraping at her own scales until a small scattering of them fell. The humanoid figure waiting by her took the smallest of them, and it was still as big as his hand. He held it over Nerra's chest right above her heart, then pushed it down against the flesh there.

Even as he did it, Nerra could feel the magic that flowed in from Shadr. She'd been able to feel Shadr's thoughts before, but now, it felt as though she was connected to something even greater, the whole of dragon kind seeming to reside within her. Nerra cried out as the scale started to fuse with her flesh, a dark patch against the blue of the rest of her. She screamed with it, and she saw...

Images flooded into Nerra, and she knew that they were memories, but not Shadr's memories. This was something deeper, and through the link Nerra now had she understood that it was something shared between all dragons, the way a species that rarely lived to see its young managed to spread its knowledge.

Nerra saw a world where dragons soared in the skies. She saw kingdoms beneath, but they were not kingdoms ruled by humans. The dragons ruled, because they were the most powerful, their very beings blended with the magic of the world. Nerra saw scaled folk below, both lesser and Perfected. She saw humans too, and she knew that they served. Those who obeyed were prosperous and knew peace. Those who betrayed their rulers became food, serving in the only way they were fit to.

She saw the moment when they rose up, fighting to overthrow the order of things. In the depths of the shared memory, she knew that it *should* have been a brief fight, should have meant only destruction for those who fought. Yet the dragons had reckoned without the human-things' capacity to learn and to grow. They had learned the ways of magic, and the ways of metal. They forged tools with which to fight, with which to *murder* the dragons and their blood. Nerra felt each death as if it were her own in that moment, felt blades sliding into flesh, and she screamed afresh with them.

She saw the war playing out below her, the humans spreading out, driving the dragons back, destroying and forgetting the land that had once been the heart of their empire. She saw the moment when magic and flame had gouged the Slate in between the Northern and Southern kingdoms, saw dragons brought down by sorcery when all of magic should have been theirs. She saw two of the three kingdoms fall to men, the third given over to jungle and ruins and fire. She saw dragons' deaths through a hundred pairs of eyes, and each hurt as much as the last.

When Nerra came back to herself, she was crying tears that slid from the scales of her skin. She could feel the thoughts of all the other dragons around her. Shadr was first among them, though. Shadr was hers, and she was Shadr's.

"What was that?" Nerra asked the dragon queen.

It is what was, the dragon replied. *Now, it is time for what will be.*

"And what is that?" Nerra asked.

Shadr reared up, breathing flame high into the sky. Around her, the other dragons did the same, answering their queen's display with their own.

Now, we take back what is ours.

Chapter Sixteen

The water battered at Greave as he clung to his makeshift raft. Everywhere he looked, the ocean spread out, waves climbing and falling high enough that their peaks seemed like mountains. It was all Greave could do to hang on, determined not to give in, not to die out here before he had done all he had come to do.

He had to help Nerra. Greave clung to that thought as tightly as he clung to the raft.

How long had he been out there? It was hard to keep track of the passage of time here. Worse, Greave had no idea where he was, even though he'd stared at maps and charts back in the castle's library to try to prepare for the journey to Astare. With no landmarks, and no land, there was no way to tell which way Royalsport lay. He'd been spun around so many times that it was hard even to judge which way the shores of the Northern Kingdom lay.

Greave lay on his back as the rolling of the waves continued, staring up at the sky as he tried to think. He rolled over onto one side, and that was when he saw it: a sliver of land on the horizon, not broad enough to fill it, but still more than big enough to give him hope.

Taking his makeshift paddle, he started to row toward it.

It seemed to take forever, the size and power of the waves making Greave's raft feel like ... well, like it was a tiny raft up against the full power of the ocean. Greave had read sailors' accounts before he'd set out north, had even experienced storms on the boat to Astare, but this was different, because he had no one to help him, no crew to guide his makeshift vessel in the direction it was meant to go.

Even so, Greave paddled as hard as he could, trying to gain ground stroke by stroke, determined to make it.

The island grew larger ahead of him, little by excruciating little. It went from a mere line on the horizon to an island that stood up from the ocean in a wash of green and brown against the blue around it. It was larger than Greave had thought at first; not on the scale of something like Leveros, but still big enough that it might have taken a whole day to cross it from one end to the other.

Greave kept paddling, struggling to get closer.

As he did, he felt the sea stop fighting him, the waves pushing his raft in toward the shore, accelerating him toward it, so that by the time it struck the sand of a beach, it was enough to throw Greave from his vessel up onto the shore.

From somewhere, he found the strength to pull his raft up above the tide line. His strength ran out after that, though, and he collapsed on the shore, breathing hard while the world around him slowly stopped spinning.

It seemed like an age before Greave was able to pull himself up to a sitting position and look around the beach on which he'd landed. It was small, just a strip of sand against the rest of it punctuated by driftwood and seaweed. Gulls landed here and there, pecking at shells they found. One looked at Greave as if trying to contemplate how long it would be before it could try eating him. Greave shooed it away.

The rest of the island seemed green and verdant. The air was cool, suggesting that he might have drifted further north from Astare, but he knew that was no real guide. The trees in the forest *looked* like the normal kind he might have found back home, but honestly, Greave could barely tell oak from chestnut or elm. He needed Nerra for that.

Or Aurelle. That thought caught Greave by surprise, but he wasn't sure *why* he was surprised. He hadn't been able to stop thinking about her all the time that he'd been caught on the ocean, wondering where she was, and how close to Royalsport she'd gotten by now.

Greave shook his head, trying to clear thoughts of Aurelle from his mind. It didn't work, but at least it pushed them back behind other, more urgent concerns. He was on an island, and he didn't know if anyone else was here. He didn't have any food with him, or shelter, or any of the other things that he was sure were needed to survive on an island.

He understood the things that he needed in theory, because he'd read books about those who had survived in the wild. He needed to find fresh water, or make it. De Halt's evaporation method came to mind, but for that, he would need a fire. How did someone go about making a fire when alone on an island?

Greave stood, combing the beach for wood that might work for a fire. It took him at least a couple of minutes to realize that with the wood still wet from the ocean, there was no way that it would burn. Greave dragged it up above the tide line anyway, where it might dry out, then set off toward the trees of the island's interior to try to find drier wood.

He found some, and then tried to work out how to start a fire. He had a flint and steel, so he collected kindling the way it had said to in Vanbert's *Methods of the Forest*. It seemed to take forever to light it, even then. Greave sat beside the resulting blaze, letting it dry him out little by little, warming him.

He reached into his tunic, taking out the scrap of parchment on which Hillard had written the processes to create his cure for the scale sickness. Some of them seemed far too complex right then, requiring fractional distillation over an oil flame and the use of dangerous reagents. Greave had a fire, and little else.

He had a list of ingredients though. Most were common, simple things that might be found anywhere. Others ... what was dark lily? Where could he find powdered amber from a lightning-struck tree? No, Greave knew that he couldn't think like that, because the moment he started to, he would be lost. He had his list. He scanned it again.

One ingredient stood out: devil's breath seaweed, dried across a fire. Greave was sure he had read a book on the properties of kelp and other sea plants once, with illustrations that had seemed to bring it all to full, horrible life. He sat there, determined to remember, delving into the storehouse where it seemed to him that everything he had ever read sat waiting.

A hazy image came to mind, of a kind of seaweed that was red and bulbous, with distinctive frayed edges to its fronds. Greave started to comb the beach again, lifting strands of weeds while the gulls looked on in case he turned up anything they could eat. He tossed scraps aside, this one for being the wrong color, that one for looking too waxy. Maybe the kind he wanted wasn't even found here, wherever *here* was.

Then he saw it, down on the sands near a rock pool. Greave actually whooped with joy in a way that shocked even himself. He snatched it up and carried it back to his fire, working out after a little thought that if he arranged sticks to make cross frames, he could suspend the seaweed from them near the fire, drying it slowly.

"I can do this," he said out loud, even though the seaweed was the simplest of the ingredients he needed. "I can *do* this."

He would find everything he needed, and not stop until he did. He would find a way to cure Nerra, whatever it took. Now, it was just a question of getting off the island.

Finding the seaweed seemed to have galvanized something in Greave though. His father and his brothers had always thought that his book learning would never amount to anything of use to the kingdom, but now, Greave knew that it was everything he could need.

Surely he'd read a book on building a more seaworthy boat at least *once?*

For now, the seaweed was enough, and Greave knew he had other priorities. He needed to make shelter, and try to purify some water to get rid of its salt. He would need to find food, and then actually work out where he was. Perhaps when the stars came out that night, he could construct some way to track them, and compare them to what he knew of the world. Even looking at the sun at dawn or sunset would give Greave an idea of where home lay.

He could do this. No matter how long or strange the list of ingredients was for the cure, Greave would find a way to locate them all. Perhaps he was the only one who could. Maybe Aurelle had been right when she'd said that he was special to be able to do all of this.

Why? Why did he keep thinking of her? She had betrayed him, lied to him about everything, and yet Greave couldn't stop himself from thinking about her. He wished that she were there, and not just because she would probably already have worked out a way off the island, or hunted down wild game to eat, or something equally direct. He wished that she were there so that he could look her in the eyes, and tell her that he loved her, and just be *near* her.

Greave didn't know where she was now, any more than he knew where he was. Wherever she was on her way back to Royalsport, he only hoped that she was safe.

CHAPTER SEVENTEEN

Aurelle felt a wash of relief as she saw Royalsport in the distance, even if it was tinged with sadness that Greave wasn't there to see it with her. She would be back soon, would be home ... and that meant that she would be able to get on with killing the ones who needed to die.

They would land at one of the coastal harbors nearest the city, and then make their way to it from there. It wouldn't take long ... except that Aurelle could see boats ahead in the distance by the harbor, and they definitely weren't those of the Northern Kingdom. They didn't even try to hide what they were, their flags the purple and red of the Southern Kingdom's armies. They'd beaten Aurelle here. Perhaps they'd been here since the moment they landed in Astare.

Then Aurelle felt the boat beneath her shift, saw the horizon move in front of her as it turned to port, veering away from Royalsport.

"What's going on?" Aurelle called out to the captain. "Why are we turning away?"

"Why do you think?" the captain shot back. "I came this way to *flee* a war zone, not to end up in one. We need to find a different place to land."

Aurelle stared at him in disbelief. "I thought when you wouldn't turn around before, that you were planning to take me where you were paid to, regardless of what I said? I thought your loyalty to the crown meant that you would follow Prince Greave's orders to the letter?"

"It's hard to be loyal to a crown that doesn't exist anymore," the captain shot back. "Do you think I can't *count*, woman? That many ships means one thing: Royalsport has fallen, and we both know Ravin won't tolerate rivals."

"Even so," Aurelle began.

"There *is* no 'even so,'" the captain snapped back. "This is *my* vessel, and *I* will decide where it goes. Now, get below while I try to work out what to do about all this."

Aurelle went, because one of the things that the House of Sighs taught was to avoid head on confrontations. Let men talk, let them command, even let them hurt you, and it was possible to learn far more than by trying to argue. She slid down belowdecks and then stopped, waiting.

A second skill that the House of Sighs taught was how to listen to what wasn't meant to be heard. There was an art to it, a way of going still and picking out sounds beyond a door or a wall, turning them into something that could be understood. Aurelle did it now, waiting and piecing it together little by little.

"...need to land somewhere else. Geertstown, maybe, or we head south and wait until it blows over."

"What about the noblewoman?"

Aurelle heard the captain laugh at that. "She's not noble. Barely even counts as a woman. Just a whore from the House."

Aurelle held back her anger at that. It was another lesson: anger could be useful, but it had to be directed. Otherwise, it put you at risk.

"We could dump her over the side," a sailor murmured above.

"Before we've even had her?" another replied. "Sounds like a waste."

"You're both idiots," the captain said. "We'll need coin. She'll be worth it to the right people. There are places in Geertstown that will pay good money for a pretty face. Or in the south. I bet there's about to be quite a market in Northern noblewomen there."

Aurelle had heard enough, and now the anger within her was a flame that she nurtured, building it into something more; something dangerous. She looked around the space of the ship's hold, taking in the crates and barrels, the oil lamp swinging above, the slope of the steps leading down.

Aurelle started to plan.

The first thing she did was to take one of her knives and loosen one of the steps down, prying it from its nails and setting it teetering. The second thing she did was to set a heavy box atop another, near the stairs' base. Then she extinguished the lamp and moved it from its hook, plunging the hold into darkness. Aurelle crouched in that darkness, letting her eyes adjust, so that even the thin threads of light coming in through the trap-door to the deck were enough. She picked her spot and settled in place.

Determination was another thing that the House taught. When a course of action was decided, it was important to act without hesitation, and without holding back. Of course, the things she was about to do ... they only taught a few how to do them. What was it in her that they'd seen to let her become this?

What would Greave say if he saw her in the dark, ready to kill?

Aurelle clutched a knife tightly in her hand. There was no choice now; nothing else to do other than this. If Greave had wanted things to be different, he should have come onto the boat with her. He shouldn't have *died*. With him in the world, there was a reason to be kind, and good, and all the things she'd pretended for his sake. Now ...

She saw the change in the light as the trapdoor opened to let in a shaft of it. It illuminated a small patch of floor, but no more than that without the additional light of the lamp. She saw a trio of them start to descend the steps; the captain and the two he'd been talking to, she guessed.

The first sailor to come down placed his foot on the step she'd loosened, and it pitched him forward, sending him tumbling to the floor of the hold with a cry and a crash. Aurelle saw him lying there, looking up as if trying to make sense of what had just happened, and then she shoved the box she'd set in place to send it toppling, crunching down onto the sailor's skull.

He deserved it, Aurelle reminded herself. *This is what you are* for. *To rid the world of men like them.*

She slipped back among the boxes as the other two came down, more wary now.

"There's no point in hiding!" the captain roared. "You'll pay for what you've done to Estan!"

Aurelle ignored him and kept up her careful movement through the darkness. She took a coin from her money pouch and picked her spot, tossing it among crates so that it clattered and scraped.

"Got you!" the other sailor with the captain said, hurrying over in the direction of the sound.

"Wait, Tien. It's a—"

The captain didn't finish his sentence before Aurelle rose up behind the sailor from the darkness, her knife sweeping out across the man's throat as she held him to her. She felt the blood spread across her hands, heard the gurgle of his breath as he died. She didn't bother hiding now, didn't dive back amongst the cover there in the hold. Instead, she stepped toward the form of the captain, still outlined in the small patch of light there.

"So you thought that you could sell me like some piece of meat," Aurelle said. "You thought that you could come down here and do what you wanted with me."

"You killed my men!" the captain snarled. He drew a long knife as thick as Aurelle's arm. For a brief moment, fear rose in Aurelle, along with more lessons from her training. Standing in front of someone with a knife was stupid. Talking when she should be striking was stupid. Don't have a fight when a knife from the dark might work. The goal was always to win, not to engage in some kind of duel.

The captain came at her, and now there was no time to think of that, only to react. Aurelle gave ground, moving among the crates, dodging back from the captain's slashes.

"I'll gut you," he promised. "I'll cut you apart."

But when you must fight, fight harder and faster than anyone would expect.

Aurelle threw herself forward, inside the sweep of the captain's next blow. She grabbed his knife arm with her free hand and started to stab with her other. In the press of such close confines, she could feel the captain's weight bearing down on her, and Aurelle didn't try to push that weight away. Space was the enemy. She felt the captain start to topple forward, and she went down with him, still stabbing again and again, because men so rarely died quickly, or quietly, or cleanly.

Only when Aurelle was sure the captain was dead did she dare to let go of her white-knuckled grip on his knife arm. She rolled the dead weight of him from her, and sucked in deep breaths while she clambered back to her feet.

She stood there, trying to think. The sensible thing to do now would be to lure the rest of them down here, one by one, and pick them off. Yet

Aurelle found herself hesitating before she tried to call for help in a rough imitation of the captain, or before she set up her next trap. The three dead in the hold had come down there specifically to hurt her; they had deserved their deaths. Even then, it felt as though Greave was looking on with disapproval at what she'd done. She could only imagine what he would think about her setting out to murder three more sailors.

What then? Aurelle stood there, looking down at her hands and the blood on them. Just the sight of it made her feel... not guilty exactly, but *something*. It also gave her an idea. Crouching, she picked up the captain's knife, holding it in one hand with her own blade in the other.

She stepped up onto the deck and saw the remaining three sailors staring at her. She knew what she must look like, blood covered and rising from the hold while the others did not. She knew how much it had to terrify the men there when she gave them a feral smile.

"Your friends are dead. Your captain is dead. Do you want to join them?"

She stared at them as they backed away. Aurelle pointed one bloody knife to the shore.

"Then get me to land, *right* now."

Chapter Eighteen

Devin stared out at the wilderness around him, trying to think, trying to work out what to do next. Master Grey's instructions to him had been clear: he needed to forge the unfinished sword here, out in the wild places, but why? Why do it here, rather than back in Royalsport?

More importantly, how?

The last time he'd forged a blade made of star metal, it had been in a forge Master Grey had set up specifically for him, the walls lined with runes that would catch and disperse power safely. They'd been needed, because again and again in the forging, Devin hadn't been able to control the magic that he'd put into the ore he'd been working with. Magic had burst from it, and Devin was sure that without the protections, it would have brought half the castle down on his head.

How was he meant to forge a blade out here, so far from anywhere?

"Do you have any ideas?" he said to Sigil. Of course, the wolf merely stayed by his side.

Devin reached his hand out to run it through the creature's fur. As soon as he touched the symbol there, he found that it was easy to reach out to sense the threads of magic around him, the wolf acting as a kind of amplifier of that connection, or perhaps a guide. Devin was the one touching that magic, but with Sigil there, it was so much easier than it had been before.

He sighed. "I guess it's something."

He picked a direction and started to ride, mounting his horse and putting his heels to its flanks. He went in the direction of the last village he'd gone through, barely more than a hamlet and still hours away. Still, Devin remembered that it had possessed a forge on the edge of the settlement, old and hardly used, but still better than nothing.

Devin guided his horse over the open ground of the waste, Sigil loping along beside him, except for moments when he darted off into the rocks and the bushes to hunt for prey. Devin watched the progress of the sun as he rode, seeing it climb across the sky with aching slowness.

Finally, he spotted the hamlet ahead. It was barely more than half a dozen buildings clustered together against the elements and the threat of bandits. There wasn't even an inn, just a hay loft near one of the farms where they'd let him bed down on the way here with the others.

Devin rode to the spot where the forge lay. It was old, and there were obvious signs of disuse. Even so, a man came out from the house nearest the forge as he approached, large and solid looking, bearded and wearing a leather apron over his peasant clothes. He looked over at Devin with initial mistrust.

"My friend and I rode through here on the way to the hills that way," Devin said, with a nod in the direction he'd just come from.

"Aye," the man said with a shrug.

"Now I'm back," Devin said.

"Aye."

The villager didn't seem to be about to offer up anything more than that. On another day, Devin might have just ridden on, found a spot to sleep under the stars, and left it at that.

"I need a forge," he said.

Now the man showed a glimmer of interest. "If your horse has thrown a shoe, I reckon I can fix it."

Devin looked around the forge, at the badly cared for tools, the forge fire itself looking as if it might come apart with too much work on it.

"I don't need my horse shod," he said, "and if I did, I could do it. I need to use your forge."

"*You* want to use *my* forge?" the man said.

Devin got down from his mount. He took out a pouch from his saddlebags. There was still money in it, because that was just one more way that Sir Twell had made sure that they were well prepared. Thoughts of the dead knight made a lump rise in Devin's throat.

"I want to use your forge, and I want a place to sleep, and I need food," Devin said. He started to count out coins onto the edge of the forge's stones.

"I might be able to do that," the villager said. He looked over to Sigil. "That's a big dog."

"He's a wolf. Leave him alone and he'll not hurt anyone. The same goes for me. No one is to disturb me."

"I'm not to come into my own forge?" the man said, in obvious disbelief.

Devin nodded. He didn't try to explain that any disruption might see a burst of magic that could kill them both. He doubted that it would exactly make the other man friendlier. "Of course, I could go to the next village, or the one after that..."

"No need for that," the man said. His hand darted out to snatch up the coins. "Truth is, I don't use the forge that much. My da was the real smith, and folk...just expected that I'd know what to do."

Devin had guessed some of that, just from the state of the forge. At least it meant that he might be left alone, when no real smith would let a stranger just use his forge like that.

He waited for the villager to go out of sight, and then turned his attention to the forge. It was cold and unused today, which meant that he could start to clean it out, taking a shovel from nearby and clearing what had to be months at least of grime and molten slag from it. Where there were cracks, he started to repair them with stones.

He set out the fragments of the unfinished sword along the edge of the forge, looking at them together, imagining what would need to be done. It wasn't just a case of welding pieces together; the metal would have to be melted down together to form a new billet for him to beat a blade out of. He would have to shape that and harden it, quench it and grind it. There was a lot of work there, even before he *thought* about the fact that he was working with star metal.

He looked at the star metal with more than normal sight then, taking in the ways that each fragment of the blade seemed to have been worked with channels for magic, each one a conduit for something different. One fragment seemed to scream its sharpness to his touch, while another spoke to him of flames, a third of cold. One had hints of protection in it, another death written in every strand. The last seemed designed to bind it all together, but there was something flawed in that binding, something that couldn't hold.

Devin knew all of that, and didn't know how he knew, except that it was magic.

When it came to that, Devin could only hope that he had the skills he needed. He sat cross-legged in the middle of the forge space, reaching out for the magic around him. He reached out for Sigil too, feeling the wolf's fur under his hand and the improvement in the connection that came with it.

This wasn't like calming a storm. Now, it was more like building a fortress, or maybe digging the drainage for a field. Devin needed to make channels in the magic itself that would let it run away from the forge as he worked, so that not too much would be in the metal at once. At first, that seemed easy enough to do around the anvil and the forge fire, but the rest of it was simply too much. The protections slid away even as Devin put them into place. Even those on the anvil started to fade as he lost concentration. There was no way he could do it *and* put magic into the star metal.

No wonder Master Grey had worked the stones with runes. Probably, those had served as ways to anchor the magic. Taking a chisel, Devin tried to remember the shape of the runes he'd seen, but maybe that wasn't the point. He *knew* the shapes the magic was making, the channels and the whorls designed to dissipate power. He could see them beneath his hands as he started to build the patterns again.

Devin set his chisel above the stone where he'd put the first of them, and started to tap with a hammer. It left no more than a scratch upon the stone, but a scratch seemed to be enough, when combined with his will and his magic. It locked the pattern into the stone, and now it didn't fade.

Devin moved onto the next part of the pattern, and the next. He carved his makeshift runes into every surface he could find, tapping with his hammer and chisel, changing the forge little by little so that it would let power run off safely. Devin hoped so, anyway. He was all too aware that Master Grey had probably had years to construct his own web of workings under the castle. This was probably enough only to guide the natural run-off of the forging process.

If Devin truly slipped, and magic burst through all this, he doubted that it would even begin to hold. The magic he used would lash out, and he would be lucky to live. The whole hamlet would be.

That just meant that he couldn't make any mistakes.

Was that why Master Grey had made him forge the sword for the wedding? Had he known that this moment would come? Had he wanted to be sure that Devin would be prepared when it did? He'd said that it was preparation for working with star metal, but if it had just been a question of bringing it back to the castle, he could have stood over Devin while he worked on this blade. Maybe he'd always been meant to finish the unfinished sword out here, away from the world.

Devin knew that with Master Grey, it was better not to speculate. Instead, he started to pack the forge, setting down kindling, then sticks, then charcoal. He lit it with a flint and steel, started to work the bellows by hand. He'd learned *that* lesson, at least. Still, he put in small flickers of magic as he worked, making sure that the flames had more to them than heat.

He would have only one chance to forge the sword as it should be, and when failure might mean death, Devin was determined to do it right.

CHAPTER NINETEEN

Lenore sat in her rooms, trying to remain composed in spite of the fear that threaded through her, threatening to overwhelm her. The castle had fallen, and Lenore had been sure that they would all be slaughtered, that the soldiers would fall on them like a pack of wolves. Instead, they had merely forced them all back into their rooms and walked the halls, declaring the new order with their presence.

Now that the castle had fallen, things were very different. It didn't feel safe in the way it had before. Lenore had seen the looks that Ravin's men had been giving her, the looks of terror among the palace's staff.

Erin stood by her side, but her sister looked different now. Her armor was hidden, along with her spear. Neither of them wanted her recognized as the one who had been moving through the streets, killing Ravin's troops. She was dressed in simple, dark clothes now, the only weapon close to her an eating knife. She looked nervous like that, as if missing the presence of her weapons.

Odd had changed into simple elegant clothes of gray cotton and silk, although he'd kept his sword. He looked almost as uncomfortable as Erin did.

"This is not the man I want to be anymore," Odd said.

"It's necessary," Lenore said. A lot of things were necessary right now, either because the new regime commanded them, or because they were all scared of what the soldiers might do next.

"I know it's necessary," Odd said. "But still..."

"Have either of you seen Finnal?" Lenore asked.

Odd and Erin both shook their heads. Where was her husband? Had he been caught up in the fighting? Was he alive or dead? Lenore didn't know, and not knowing only added to the sense of chaos that was brewing in her.

Her mother was in her own rooms, apparently as safe as she was, but she didn't know what had happened to Finnal. The same questions could be applied to Orianne, her maid, her friend. She had been out in the city when the attack came, off about the task Lenore had set for her. Lenore could only hope that she had found somewhere safe to shelter. Again, sitting there not knowing only added to Lenore's feelings of helplessness, until she was sure that she might burst with them if she didn't find some kind of answers.

There was no way to find her right now, but at least there were other things she could do.

"I'm going to find my husband," Lenore said.

"Is that a good idea?" Erin asked. "You'd be safer here."

"I'm sick of just being safe," Lenore said. "It feels...it feels like someone is dangling a sword over my head right now as it is. Walking around the castle won't make things worse."

Before the other two could object, Lenore stood and walked to the doors to her rooms. She flung them open and strode out, with Erin and Odd struggling to keep up in her wake. There was a pair of guards in the corridor in the purple and red of the Southern Kingdom, the Three Kingdoms now. They stepped in front of them, hands going to their swords.

"It is forbidden for more than two of the inhabitants of the castle to walk the halls together," one said.

"I was just trying to locate my husband," Lenore said, in her most placating tone.

"It is forbidden for more than two of the inhabitants of the castle—"

"Yes, we heard you," Erin said. "I'll go back. Odd can go with you."

"Stay safe," Lenore said, hugging her. Erin was going back in the direction of her rooms though, so there was no reason to think that her sister might be in danger. So far, doing as they were commanded seemed to be enough to keep people safe.

"The carrying of any weapon larger than a dagger beyond any of the rooms of the castle is also forbidden," one of the guards said, with a nod toward Odd's sword. Lenore froze at those words, because she wasn't sure how the former monk would react.

To her surprise, he laughed. "Oh, this?" He drew the sword in one smooth movement, and it blurred through the air in a figure eight pattern that had the guards starting to draw their own blades. Almost as quickly as he had drawn it, though, he slammed it back into its sheath. "I had quite forgotten that I was wearing it. Erin, would you take my sword back with you, please?"

He tossed the sword to Erin, who caught it expertly and turned to leave.

"It is not as if I need a sword to kill," Odd said, still with the same smile on his face as he and Lenore started to walk past the guards. Their faces were still caught in shock and surprise.

It was the tiniest of victories, and Lenore had no doubt that they would end up paying for it later, but for now, Odd startling the guards made her feel a little safer.

They set off in the direction of the rooms that she supposedly shared with Finnal now, and when Lenore opened the doors, she found him standing there, talking to a servant.

"Finnal!" Lenore said. She threw herself forward, sweeping him into an embrace. "You're alive!"

"Of course I'm alive," Finnal said. He pulled back from her and managed a smile. "I'm glad you're safe, of course."

"But where have you been?" Lenore asked.

"I had some … business in the city," Finnal said. "It made getting back difficult. And obviously since then, I have been trying to understand how things are, sending messages, adjusting to the … changes."

How could anyone make an invasion sound like it was just one more political shift to be ridden out?

"And in all this, you didn't have time to see me?" Lenore demanded.

She caught the moment when Finnal glanced across to Odd. He seemed to take a moment to think. "Things have been moving very quickly, Lenore. It's very important to position ourselves to survive within the new regime."

"To position ourselves to survive?" Lenore said, unable to keep the emotion out of her voice. "King Ravin had me kidnapped. He's responsible for the deaths of my brother and father. You think he won't slaughter us too?"

Couldn't Finnal see that this wasn't some normal thing, something to deal with calmly? People had *died.*

"I doubt that he will," Finnal said. "My father has always said that King Ravin is a reasonable man. When he unified the Southern Kingdom, he was quick to incorporate the local rulers into his governance."

"You're making this sound like...like some kind of business deal," Lenore said.

"Oh, I have no doubt that Ravin will want to make us squirm a little," Finnal said. "But I suspect that he would rather have us stand as witnesses to his reign than simply kill us. Frankly, if he wanted to do that, he would have done it the moment his troops entered the castle."

When Finnal wasn't there. When it had just been Lenore. Her husband had stayed away, leaving her to her fate. Lenore had to fight to keep any kind of composure on her face right then.

"I...I can see that you have a lot to do," she said. "Will I see you later?"

"Yes, of course," Finnal said. "You are my wife, after all. Assuming that King Ravin doesn't demand you for his own."

He actually said that with a laugh, as if it were a joke, and not something to send terror flooding through Lenore's heart. Lenore barely staggered from the room before she did something stupid, like screaming at him. As it was, she made it halfway back to her rooms before she all but collapsed with the effort of not giving in to her fear. Odd was there though, catching her by the elbow, supporting her as elegantly as if they were both out for a stroll.

"Odd," she said, whispering it because she didn't know who would be listening now. "Can you do something for me?"

"Anything," Odd said.

"I need you to find a messenger for me, someone I can trust absolutely."

It was clear from Odd's expression that it wasn't what he'd thought she would ask, but even so, he nodded. "I will."

"I'll be in my rooms," Lenore said. She hurried back to them. Erin was there, standing on a balcony, looking out over the city. Lenore went to join her. There were a few fires in the outer city, but for the most part the stillness and silence of the city were terrifying. There were soldiers marching in the streets now, moving in formation, making it clear that they owned Royalsport. There were work gangs in place down at the sites of the old bridges, rebuilding them little by little. Other gangs seemed to be moving under the gaze of the troops, moving goods down to waiting carts. The market was open, but there were troops everywhere among it, clearly controlling everything that was taking place.

"It's going to get worse," Erin said.

Lenore nodded. There was no way that it could do anything else. "We have to find a way to survive, together."

"Together," Erin agreed, taking Lenore's hands in hers. "I promise I won't let them hurt you."

Lenore knew that her sister meant it, but she also wasn't sure what her sister could do against the full might of Ravin's armies.

"I know," Lenore said. She went over to a small table, taking out a scrap of parchment and a quill. "For now, I have a letter to write."

She smoothed out the parchment and tried to work out what to say. What *could* she say, at a time like this?

Dearest Devin, she wrote, *I have to write this, have to let you know what's happening. Royalsport has fallen to the Southern Kingdom. I am safe for now, along with Erin and the others, but Ravin rules here, and his armies fill the city. Master Grey held things for a while, but he is gone now. I do not know what is happening here anymore. I only hope you are safe. I do not know what else to hope, whether you are coming back or staying safe away from here, but I do know that I wish you were here beside me.*

It didn't seem like a tenth of what she wanted to say to him, but it was all Lenore could think to put down.

Odd was back there then, with a man who looked as though he might have been a soldier once. The man fell to one knee.

"My lady," he said. "I'm told that you have a task for me."

"I need you to get a message beyond the city," Lenore said. She folded the parchment and put it in the man's hand. "Do you know Devin, the boy who was Master Grey's student?"

The man nodded. "I have met him. I heard he headed north."

"I need you to find him," Lenore said. "There are passages to leave the castle, or maybe you could do it in disguise. Go north, seek him out. Deliver this."

"I will," the messenger promised.

He went to go, and even as he did, he passed a couple of King Ravin's men, who came in as easily as if they owned the whole castle. Lenore guessed that they did, now.

"We bring a command from King Ravin," one of them said.

Lenore was barely paying attention, all her focus on the messenger who had just left. If they realized what he was carrying, they were probably all dead. For now, it seemed that the men were focused on their own message.

"What command?" she asked.

"He commands your presence, to swear fealty to him as Emperor of the Three Kingdoms."

CHAPTER TWENTY

Ravin stood at the head of a procession of the nobles of his newly acquired kingdom, standing before them resplendent, dressed for the occasion in the purple of his robes of state, his crown of platinum atop his head. He smiled with satisfaction at the sight of so many of those who had stood against him before there, forced to participate in this moment by the presence of the soldiers who flanked them.

His men had drawn them from around the castle and its grounds: all those who might have stood against him. He wondered how many of them thought they were being led to their deaths. Ravin enjoyed that.

The former queen, Aethe, was there toward the middle, along with her daughters. Vars was toward the rear. Ravin had made a point of putting them there, to make it clear to them that the old order of precedence was no more. The women didn't seem to care, but he could see the anger on the coward king's face.

"Begin," he ordered a herald beside him. The man raised a horn to his lips and blew a single long note. Together, their procession started to move down into the city.

The signs of the new order stood all around, in Ravin's troops keeping control of the streets, in the officials moving from noble house to noble house to take a tithe from each. It was more orderly than sacking the city in a rush, and it did far more to establish who ruled here.

Ravin turned his attention to the city's great Houses, each standing above a district of the city, each with its traditional role to play in the order of things. Ravin intended to make full use of each. The House of Weapons was already belching out black smoke again, as Ravin wished it to. His armies would still need weapons to maintain order, and would use its training spaces to practice their skills.

The House of Scholars stood with its towers flying Ravin's colors now. It would write histories of his glory, provide his empire with knowledge that had been hidden for generations. Perhaps with their knowledge, his colonies in Sarras would even succeed.

The House of Merchants stood blocky and secure above the markets. Ravin was having his men take their share to return to the south with, but it was not all of it; it did not need to be. It was better to keep everything running, making money for him. This was not some foreign land to raid anymore: it was his kingdom.

As for the House of Sighs with its silks and its painted façade above the entertainment district... well, his men would need ways to enjoy themselves, especially now that the war was all but done. An army with nothing to do needed distractions, so that it didn't become dangerous.

Ravin led the way down through the noble district, and even though his men had not completed the bridges yet, he led the way across the stream bed there. Ravin was a warrior, and he had come prepared with a fighter's boots. He turned on the far bank and looked back; he enjoyed watching the faces of the nobles there as they had to cross the mud in their courtly shoes and slippers.

He enjoyed making them do this, too, leading them through the streets of the city, through the richer districts and the slums. It wasn't just because his men pushed the common folk out into the street to cheer. It was because with every step he took, it was like he was claiming another stride of the city's streets for his own.

He watched them as he passed, the people cheering there with frightened eyes. They were wondering how their lives would change, if there would be men kicking down their doors to take their daughters in the night, or forcing them to work to death in the mines, or simply stealing all they had.

And the answer to that fear was that it would happen if Ravin willed it to happen. They were his now, to do with as he wished. The nobles too. He glanced round at them; he wondered if they truly understood the way things were now. They soon would. The truth was that life would change far more for most of them than the common folk.

He led the way to the square in the city he had picked out for this moment. There were crowds there as well, of course, but they were of the merchants and the scholars, the more noble kinds of people rather than the commoners. These were the ones who needed to see how things were changing, and who needed to understand that they had no choice in what was happening.

At the center of the square, Ravin's men had constructed a gallows, with a headsman's block set upon it. His great sword, Heartsplitter, stood next to the block, freshly sharpened. Ravin looked around, knowing that the sight of it would bring back all the fears that had been there before.

He mounted the gallows, and behind him he could hear the gasps and the muttering, but his men would hold those there in place. Disarmed as they were, there was no way for them to fight.

He stood before the crowd and addressed them, staring out at them, daring anyone to make a sound in this moment. He knew he looked every inch the ruler there, because he had orchestrated this to perfection. People would remember this day for as long as they lived.

Many of them would even see sundown.

He stood there, watching their fear, waiting for the right moment to speak.

"I am Ravin," he said. "And from this moment, I am Emperor of the Three Kingdoms. The world that you know belongs to me. I need no coronation, no ceremony beyond this, because I do not hold this land by the grace of the gods, or men, or history. I hold it because I have conquered what should always have been mine."

He rested a hand on the hilt of his sword, letting the words sink in, taking in the crowd's fearful murmuring.

"I am willing to be merciful," he said. "I am here to rule, not to destroy. You will have your places in my kingdom, if you are willing to swear fealty to me."

"And what if we don't?" a nobleman called out.

Ravin nodded, and two of his Quiet Men, hidden among the nobles, moved in. They dragged the man forward, even as he tried to protest.

"I am Lord Harman! My allies are—"

"Bring him," Ravin said, pointing to the block.

"No!" the nobleman said, but the Quiet Men dragged him into place anyway. They tied him to the block, and Ravin lifted his blade. "Please, I'll swear fealty!"

"I do not give second chances," Ravin said, and cut down. Heartsplitter severed the man's head cleanly, blood spilling, a gasp from the crowd showing their reaction to the instant of brutality. Ravin heard the gasps from the crowd around, the ones that he had been waiting for, had known that this moment would produce. A king who could not guess at the emotions of those he ruled did not rule for long.

"Is there anyone who will swear fealty now?" he demanded. He looked out over the crowd of nobles, as if he were doing it at random and not scanning the faces there one by one. "Is there anyone who will be first, who will show the way to the others here?"

He picked out the man he was looking for, the one he'd had careful discussions with before this. "Finnal, son of Viris, step forward."

The young man strode to the gallows and dropped to one knee before Ravin with smooth elegance.

"I swear my loyalty to you, Emperor Ravin, and that of my father."

Ravin held out a hand to him, pulling him to his feet. "You will hold all your lands from me? You will uphold my laws, and fight my enemies?"

"I will," he promised, as he had already promised in private.

That was the start of it. They started to come up one by one as Ravin pointed to them, and the ones who hesitated were dragged forward to the block for Heartsplitter to do its work. Soon, the gallows were red with their blood, but there were fewer than Ravin had thought there would be. They knew they were beaten.

He pointed to Queen Aethe, to her daughters. "Queen Aethe, I see you there in the crowd. Will you speak? You are surrounded by your nobles. What say you?"

"What would you have me say?" Queen Aethe replied. "When I am surrounded by your guards?"

"Bring them."

His men surrounded them, forcing them towards the gallows. Already, he could see the youngest daughter, Erin, looking for a way out. Ravin had been careful to ensure that there was none. The three of them were pushed toward the gallows, up onto it, before Ravin. He saw the older daughter look toward Finnal, but Ravin knew that there would be no help there.

"Aethe, the times have not been kind to you," Ravin said.

"The times, or you?" the former queen shot back.

Ravin turned his attention to the daughters.

"Princess Lenore," he said. "You *are* as lovely as ever. I had hoped that you would be waiting for my pleasures in my hunting lodge. Yet I suppose this brings you more conveniently to hand."

"I don't plan on being to your, or anyone's, hand," Lenore said.

"I'm not in the habit of giving up my claims on things, or people," Ravin said.

"I was under the impression that you had just accepted my husband's fealty," Lenore countered.

Ravin could hear the fear there, and that was all he was looking for.

"Perhaps. Perhaps not." He turned his attention to the youngest. "And Princess Erin," he said. "My men are telling tales of a girl who led the fighting in the city, killing many. I wonder, if I bring you to them, will they recognize you?"

"If I'd fought anyone, they wouldn't be alive to talk about it," the girl said, but her mother caught her arm.

"Oh, don't fear," he said to the former queen. "I have no reason to look so closely. For now."

He took a moment for those words to sink in.

"You know what I require," Ravin said to Aethe. "And you know what will happen if you refuse. But I say this too. If you do not kneel, I will kill your daughters. I will gut them and let you listen to their screams."

These were the moments he enjoyed most as a ruler; the moments when people knew that they had no choice but to obey. He let the weight of his eyes rest on them, let them see the truth of what would happen if they did not submit.

She knelt; how could she not? The others stared at her in shock, but she tugged at their sleeves, and they knelt beside her, as Ravin had known that they would. He smiled in triumph.

Ravin turned to address the crowd. "These ones used to think that they had power here," he said. "I will show them that they have no power. I will let them live, because I am merciful."

He turned back to Aethe, moving close to her, whispering. "And you will watch everything that I do in the kingdom, to your family. You will watch, and you will know that you are powerless to do anything to stop me, that you always were." He let a smile spread across his face, slow and cruel. "Perhaps I will have Erin killed. Perhaps I will claim sweet Lenore as my own. Or perhaps I will simply kill *her.* Either way, you will live, knowing that there is *nothing* you can do about it."

Chapter Twenty One

The House of Sighs had always been about balancing things, but Meredith wasn't sure if that was even possible now. How was she supposed to balance out any of the things that were currently happening in Royalsport? People were coming to her with reports, waiting for ideas, waiting for her to *help*. Those reports sat in a pile on the solid oak of her desk, and Meredith knew that she would have to burn them or hide them soon, so that they wouldn't be found. For now though, all she could do was sit there and listen.

"There have been more soldiers in," one of her girls said. She had a bruise above one eye that was almost, but not quite, disguised with makeup. "They're rough, and half of them don't pay."

"That will settle down," Meredith said. Even though she wasn't sure she believed it, she knew she had to try to give the girl help. "We will send gifts to Emperor Ravin, followed by politely bringing up what has happened. He will see that the House of Sighs makes money, and he will not want his men reducing his share."

It wasn't what she wanted to do. There had always been those who paid for such things, of course, and with some of the highest nobles it had been impossible to strike back, but in general, anyone who abused her people quickly found themselves hurt in return. To do that now, though, would only invite retribution from Ravin's army. She sighed.

"In the meantime, the most we can do is try to keep our ears open for secrets. Those will have value in this new world, the same way they did in the old. Do you understand?"

The woman nodded, and Meredith could see the determination there. In truth, that was what she'd been hoping to achieve, because that determination might help her to endure where she might not have before. There was so much to endure right now, for anyone trapped in the city with Ravin's men. The woman stood and left Meredith's chambers, leaving the mistress of the House of Sighs alone with her thoughts.

Meredith wished that she could have offered her more than vague hopes that would probably mean nothing. The trouble was that her position so often required a strange balance of hard and soft, kindness and cold-heartedness. She cared about all those who served within the House, as *she* had served, but at the same time she knew that her job often entailed encouraging the women and men there into situations that they might not want otherwise. And that was just the ones who served the House's patrons, not the ones who were trained to unearth secrets.

One of those came to her next, a young woman who looked like a courtesan until she crossed the threshold of Meredith's chambers, but whose movements changed then to something with the grace of a fighter. She was slender and dark-haired, wearing a velvet dress that probably had plenty of pockets for weaponry.

"Ravin's Quiet Men are throughout the city," she said, in a bleak voice. "They're making it harder to help people, because any starving man begging for food might be one of them."

"Do you think I hadn't guessed that one, Sula?" Meredith asked with a wan smile. "Where he goes, they go, although I'm not sure he's worked out the full purpose of this House yet. He would have called me to him to demand allegiance if he had."

"Or to kill you," Sula pointed out. She'd always been direct in a way that most of her girls weren't. It made her suited to some of the more violent actions the House took, but less to the rest of it. "He would probably want to install one of his own people to control the House."

Meredith shook her head, even though the fear of that was there. "I have too many secrets for that to be a good idea, and he'll want direct control, the way he does with his Quiet Men. More likely, he'll take me to his bed, to prove how much more powerful he is than me."

"Don't they all?" Sula snorted.

King Godwin hadn't. He had been a king who had treated her House with respect, when others had derided it. He'd understood its purposes.

Ravin would probably understand those purposes too, but he would want to assert control. Meredith was not looking forward to that.

"His soldiers are proclaiming new laws," Sula said. "There are to be curfews for all non–Southern born subjects, and restrictions on large gatherings."

"So no parties beyond the House," Meredith said, with a shrug that was deliberately disarming. "If anything, it will force people to us for their enjoyment."

"We'll need a lot. There are more people coming to us, looking to join us."

Meredith nodded, as if she didn't know that. Of course there would be new servants for the House, because they had nowhere else to go.

"Food supplies are starting to dry up," Meredith said, by way of an explanation. "Ravin's armies will eat the city bare until he moves them on to the next phase of conquering the kingdom." She put a finger to a scrap of paper on her desk. "I'm also told that his men are starting to transport crops south to spread among the kingdom there. It will both proclaim his victory and feed his people."

"Aren't *we* supposed to be his people now?" Sula asked. "The House of Sighs serves the ruler, and Ravin rules now."

Meredith cocked her head to one side. "The House serves the balance of the kingdom, and the world. Usually, that accords with the king, but tell me, Sula, what's balanced about people starving in the streets, or being dragged from their homes, or being crushed under new laws?"

The other woman hesitated a moment or two. "If you want Ravin dead…"

Meredith put a finger to Sula's lips, stopping her. "Don't say it. Don't even think it. It's not just that anyone who tried it would probably die doing it; it's what happens then. There's an army in the city. Without their emperor to hold them together, they'd burn Royalsport."

"They'd fall to fighting among themselves," Sula countered. "You know that the South is only unified by Ravin's strength."

She was right, and not right, all at once. Yes, Ravin had carved a kingdom out of disparate pieces that always seemed to be on the brink of civil war, but that didn't make them less dangerous. The Southern Kingdom would fall apart without him, but not, she suspected, before it had taken revenge on wherever killed him.

"We hold back for now," Meredith instructed. "We endure. We help others to endure."

If they could. The kingdom had rarely suffered so much.

"Sometimes we all do things we don't like, for the greater good. In your case, *not* doing this is just as important."

"Will you be saying that when it's you he commands to his bed?" Sula shot back.

Meredith forced herself to stay calm. "You're overstepping, Sula. You can only see some of the pieces here."

The other woman looked as though she might say something else, but managed to stop herself. That was good, at least. She had *some* self-control. Sula nodded.

"As you say. I will return to trying to help the starving who are arriving on our doorstep."

She turned and left, her walk turning back to a courtesan's sway as she stepped beyond the door. Meredith sighed. It wasn't that she disagreed with any of the sentiments Sula had put forward. It was just ... someone like Aurelle wouldn't have needed to be told that there were other factors in play. Nor would Orianne. Meredith only hoped that those two were safe, in a time when it seemed that no one was.

It wasn't just because they might be able to help things, either, with a word in the right place in Orianne's case, or a knife, in Aurelle's. Meredith liked them both. Of course, as mistress of the House of Sighs, liking someone didn't stop her from sending them to do awful things. Just look at Aurelle with Duke Viris's plan. The truth, though, was that the House had needed his support, and the kingdom had needed a way to avoid a full civil war on Godwin's death. Helping Finnal into a position of power had seemed like the only way.

Like so many of the choices in Meredith's life, it was one that came to her tangled, the right thing mixed up with regret at the wrong methods. Her House would take in some of those who came looking for food, but they would end up serving the pleasures of those who came to it. It would seek to mitigate the worst effects of the new regime, but that would mean growing closer to it, going along with it, even *helping* it. Duke Viris feeling that he was achieving his aims for his son limited the scope for war, but it had meant manipulations that had caused good people pain. Cutting off Prince Greave's dangerous research into the scale-sickness had the potential to stop the world plunging back into old things best forgotten, but, by now, it had probably meant the life of a good man.

Meredith wondered how much the guilt of her life would weigh on her when she was eventually held in the balance by the gods. Would they understand the reasons behind it all, or just see the things that had been necessary? She took a decanter of wine from a side table, poured some, and took a sip.

She was still contemplating the successes and failures of her life when the door to her chambers opened without a knock, admitting a man dressed as a clerk of Ravin's court, purple and red edging his robes. Meredith knew a Quiet Man when she saw one. He was accompanied by a pair of soldiers.

"So," she said. She had to force her tone to stay polite, in spite of the terror she felt in that moment. "Emperor Ravin knows all about my little House?"

"He has always known, lady," the Quiet Man said. "I'm told he admires it. Now, he requires your presence."

"In his throne room?" Meredith asked.

"His private chambers."

"Of course," Meredith said, not letting anything she felt show in that moment. As she'd told Sula, sometimes they all did things they didn't want to for the greater good. "Lead the way."

CHAPTER TWENTY TWO

When Vars got back to the castle with all the others, King Ravin's men made him stand in the middle of the throne room. Just stand, and wait, with no explanation. King Ravin went off in the direction of the royal chambers, the chambers that should have been *his*, but Vars didn't dare to say so. He didn't dare to move, either. He didn't dare *anything*.

How long did they make him stand there like that? It had to be an hour or more, until his legs ached, and his bladder felt like it was going to burst. The fear was a part of that. He'd been the only one who hadn't had to swear allegiance out in the square, and Vars couldn't understand what that might mean. Was Ravin saving him for some particularly vile death? Was he waiting for his own execution?

All Vars could do was stand there and stare at the throne set at the head of the hall, great and dark and solid. Vars knew what that throne felt like, but right then, he couldn't ever imagine sitting in it again. Around him, the rest of the hall seemed different. The carpets to carefully delineate people's ranks were gone. Either Ravin intended to only allow nobles into his hall, or he simply viewed everyone else as equally beneath him.

After what seemed like forever, people started to file into the great hall. Soldiers stood at the edges, and Vars had no doubt that there would be Quiet Men in among the others who came in. There were nobles there, standing in their usual places, some of them looking as if nothing had changed. Finnal stood near the front, laughing at a joke from some friend or other. He didn't even look Vars's way.

Ravin came in some time after that, at the point when Vars's legs had started to shake with the strain of standing there. He had a woman with him Vars thought he recognized from the House of Sighs. She knelt by the throne as Ravin took it, looking humiliated to be doing so, but clearly having no choice. Ravin set his great sword on the other side, resting against the throne as if a reminder of how it had come to be his. He lowered himself into the seat, looking out over the room.

Vars squirmed as Ravin sat there, his eyes boring into Vars's.

"What kind of man betrays his kingdom just to save his own life?" the new emperor asked. He addressed the room. "That's what your 'king' did. He gave away the route into the castle just so that he could live. He begged me not to kill him."

Vars wanted to shout that down, wanted to argue. Two things stopped him: he was too afraid of what Ravin might do if he did, and, of course, it was true.

"Do not look so afraid, *King* Vars," Ravin said, with a smile that made Vars shiver all the more. "I'm not just going to let you live; I'm going to let you keep your throne and your crown."

Vars frowned at that, because it seemed impossible.

"I don't understand," he said.

"I am an emperor, not just a king," Ravin replied. "I will need men under me to administer the regions that I control. I will need a king to announce the laws that I decide, and to take responsibility for any failures."

"You want a puppet," Vars said, a flash of anger coming out before he could stop it.

Ravin stood, towering over him. "Exactly."

He snapped his fingers, and servants came out, carrying a chair. It was a small mockery of the throne that sat in the hall, carved with what looked, to Vars's eyes, like scenes of Royalsport being overrun. They set it down just off the dais on which the true throne sat, and Vars could only stare at it in horror.

"You want... you want me to sit in that?"

"I do not 'want' it, King Vars," Ravin said. "I command it. Of course, if you do not want your throne, there is an alternative."

His hand went to the hilt of his sword and Vars *wanted* to be brave in that moment, *wanted* to tell Ravin that he would rather die than be humiliated in such a fashion. Instead, he found his feet moving toward the dais, and as he reached the throne at the edge he turned to sit down. The chair was uncomfortably hard, and Vars was certain that it was deliberate, just another way to remind him that he had no true power here.

Around him, he could see people's amusement written on their faces, even as they tried to hide it. They'd always thought less of him, but now they were laughing at him. Vars could see Aethe toward the back, and she seemed to be enjoying his humiliation even more than the rest of them.

"Of course," Ravin said, "you will have no real power. I will appoint suitable governors when I am not present, and you will merely be a mouthpiece who announces their policies. You will be a thing brought out for displays and festivals, a thing for children to mock in the street. Do you have any objections, King Vars?"

Vars knew that the slightest qualm on his part would result in violence, that Ravin was goading him half in the hope that he would do the stupid thing, and give him an excuse to do violence in front of the assembled crowd. Vars wouldn't give him that excuse.

"None, my emperor," he managed, in spite of his anger and his humiliation. His fear was greater.

"Really? You are such a coward that you would rather be a joke than suffer the pain of a swift death?" Ravin moved around in front of him, holding that sword of his.

"Please don't kill me," Vars said. He threw himself at Ravin's feet. He didn't care then how it looked, or that it was a complete humiliation. "Please, I'll do anything."

"Yes, I believe you will. Return to your throne, King Vars. We have the business of the court to conduct."

"Yes, my emperor."

Vars stood and returned to the hard seat of the throne. Ravin stood beside him, leaning on his sword.

"I have declarations, King Vars," he said. "You will announce them for me."

"Yes, my emperor," Vars said. He wished that he had the strength or the courage to put a knife in Ravin in that moment. He'd managed it with his father, hadn't he, when the anger had pushed him far enough? Of course, his father had been weak in that moment, only just woken. He pushed those thoughts down, knowing that Ravin would see it in his face, might kill him just for that.

"First, there is a matter of what is due to me. I will have one part in three of all wealth in the kingdom, with no exceptions. After that, I will have one part in four of every income, every year. Announce it."

With a shaking voice, Vars said the words.

"Then there is the matter of my armies and the other services of the empire. Upon their eighteenth birthday, every man and woman of the empire will spend a year in service, in the army, or in any other role that is deemed suitable for them."

Vars announced that too. By now, he could almost feel the hatred coming from the crowd of people along with their derision.

"Then, of course, there is the honorable role of my consorts," Ravin said. "In the south, families compete to provide the most beautiful of their women to serve me for a time. Clearly, in the north it will take time to establish that tradition, so the process will be managed by lottery. Thankfully, you, King Vars, have already provided me with one such."

A pair of guards escorted Lyril through the crowd. She looked as beautiful as ever, and terrified. She looked over to Vars as if he might step forward, as if he might *save* her.

"You have no objection, King Vars?" Ravin said.

"Of... of course not," Vars replied.

"No?" Ravin seemed to be caught now between enjoyment and disgust. "You truly are a worm of a man, King Vars. Announce that."

"What?" Vars said.

"Announce it," Ravin said. His hand went to his sword again. "Unless you want to die?"

"I am a worm!" Vars announced to the rest of the hall.

"Yes, you are," Ravin said, "but you are also a king, and a king should have a crown."

He snapped his fingers again, and a servant came forward holding a velvet cushion. A crown sat on it, but it was nothing like the traditional crown of the Northern Kingdom. It was still a circlet of gold, with spikes rising up above it, yet in between, the cloth of a jester's hat was there, bells sitting on the end.

Even compared to the rest of it, this felt like a humiliation. Vars could actually feel tears coming to his eyes as Ravin took it in his hands, lifting it over Vars's head.

"Look out," Ravin said. "I don't want you to forget this moment. I want you never to forget that I own you now, as surely as the lowest serf."

Vars did as he was commanded, staring out at the others. He hated them in that moment, but nowhere near as much as he hated himself. He felt Ravin settle the ludicrous, humiliating crown onto his head, and Vars's eyes were so blurred with tears that he couldn't even see anymore.

"All hail King Vars!" Ravin said, but he said it as a joke. The worst part was that all the others joined in that joke, prompted by the guards around them.

"All hail King Vars!"

Right then, Vars wished that he were dead, but he knew that things would get worse. In a kingdom like this, they would always find a way to get worse.

CHAPTER TWENTY THREE

Renard stumbled along the road toward Royalsport, not daring to stop, even to sleep, when he was sure that there would be a dragon following in his wake the moment he did. Besides, sleep brought with it nightmares of the Hidden creeping up on him with every step, and the things they might do if they caught him.

He tried to tell himself to stop it, because Renard had never been the kind of man to be consumed by fears before. He'd leapt from a waterfall, stolen from Lord Carrick's vault, double-crossed the Hidden themselves! All right, so none of those had exactly turned out perfectly, but he was still alive, wasn't he?

For now, at least.

Renard pushed on, ignoring the feeling of weakness that was spreading through his body as his strength leached into the amulet he carried. It was only a trickle, but it was a trickle that had been running since he left Geertstown. Renard felt like a bucket with a pinprick hole in it, one that was now almost empty. He didn't want to think about what would happen when it *was* empty, though; he'd seen that, and it wasn't pretty.

He kept going along the roads, through a patch of woodland. Ordinarily, he would have strolled through it, singing as he went. Well, no, strictly speaking, he would have spent the time complaining and wondering exactly how far it was to the next decent inn. Either way, he would have been confident as he went, secure in the knowledge that whatever came up, he could fight it off.

Now, he slunk through the woods as the trees hemmed him in on either side. It wasn't that he was afraid, exactly; it was more that he was all too aware of just how vulnerable he was right then. Renard felt as though he would be hard pressed to fight off a child.

Of course, it was the way of the world that looking like prey only served to attract more predators.

Renard heard them before he saw them, moving through the woods with a lack of skill and grace that made Renard almost embarrassed to be a thief. Perhaps these were soldiers, pushed into the woods by the war, or villagers with nothing better to do to keep from starving than rob their fellow men.

Ordinarily, Renard would have plunged into the woods and led them on a merry chase, probably losing them easily in the shadows. Or he'd have fought them, man to man, brave as a lion right up to the point where he decided it was better to run away again. Now, he felt too exhausted for either, which meant that he was going to have to rely on wit, charm, and the boundless depths of his likeability to survive this.

He was in so much trouble.

"Why?" he demanded of the heavens. "Why do you keep doing this to me?"

"Why does who keep doing what, old man?" A young man dressed in what looked like the tattered remains of a soldier's uniform stepped from the trees. A couple more stepped up behind Renard. The one in the lead was slender and clean shaven, while the others were burlier and bearded.

"I knew you would be soldiers," Renard said, and then paused. "Wait, 'old man'?"

"Well, you're hardly as sprightly as in your youth, are you?" the soldier replied, with a laugh. "Skin all pale, hair going gray..."

In a panic, Renard pulled his hands through the strands of his hair, dragging some in front of his face. It wasn't gray, not exactly, but instead was closer to a pale, washed out version of its usual vivid red. Apparently, the amulet was leeching the life out of even that.

"Old? It's making me *old*?"

"Might as well stab him, Hugh," one of the others said. "He's obviously mad."

Renard drew his sword at that, more on instinct than anything. "I'm not mad," he snapped back. "Probably."

"Then why are you talking to the sky?" the one who'd stepped out in front of him demanded.

"Because the gods are clearly having some kind of joke at my expense!" Renard shouted back, again as much at the sky as at the men in front of him. "First, I found myself caught trying to steal gold from Lord Carrick. Then the damn Hidden showed up to demand I work for them and find an amulet for them. Now, I'm being chased by them, and by every dragon within a dozen leagues of me."

He didn't know whether to laugh or cry as he said it; it seemed that he might be doing both.

"Like I said," the one behind him said. "Mad."

Renard spun toward him, raising his sword to cut the man down. On any other day, he would have killed all three, soldiers or not. Now, he took one halting step forward before the soldier he'd just turned his back on put both hands on his shoulders and pulled him down to the ground. Renard lost his grip on his weapon and it went skittering away into the undergrowth.

"Less of that," the leader, Hugh, said. "I've no interest in killing you, old-timer. You're harmless enough to us, and we're not murderers."

"You aren't?" Renard said, but he resisted the urge to give the men a lesson in the basic principles of banditry. This really wasn't the moment.

"It's just that a man has to do what he must to live," the leader said. "So here's what's going to happen: you're going to hand over everything you have, and then we're going to walk away, and you're going to go on wherever you're going."

"I'm off to see the sorcerer in Royalsport," Renard said, sitting up.

"I don't care. Give me everything you have, right now."

Renard sighed and tossed his coin pouch onto the woodland path.

"What's in the other pouch?" the leader of the trio said.

Renard winced just at the thought of the amulet. "You don't want that. Trust me."

"Trust *me*, I do," he shot back. He reached down to snatch the pouch from Renard's waist. Almost instantly, Renard felt the drag on his spirit ease.

He opened the pouch, taking out the eight-sided amulet and holding it up to the light. The scale at the heart of it reflected that light, along with the jewels set around the edges. Renard heard the gasp from the three soldiers.

"You think we don't want this?" the leader of the would-be bandits demanded. "I decide to let you live, and you try to hide *this* from us?"

"You really don't want to touch that," Renard said. He was trying to be polite about this, at least, since the soldier *had* said he was going to let Renard live. Compared to most of the people he'd met recently, it was a vast improvement.

"I've had enough of you telling me what I want," the soldier said. He took out his sword, so that it shone in the sunlight almost as much as the amulet. "I tried to be good about this, and you tried to trick us."

He lifted his sword over Renard, poised over his head so that for a moment, Renard could only stare at the point of it. There was no way to avoid this. Even if he dodged the first blow, the others would only come in from the sides to kill him. Renard could hear his heart hammering in his ears as the certainty that he was about to die thundered through him.

"Can't we talk about this?" he started to say, even though he knew it wouldn't do any good. He'd seen the moment when men decided to kill before, the instant when talking to them wouldn't do any good. Quite often, they'd been looking at Renard while they decided it. Usually, Renard got around the problem by running or stabbing them, but he couldn't do either now. He couldn't do anything except lie there and wait for death.

He saw the moment when it happened, saw the change in the soldier's expression. He dropped his sword, and Renard barely rolled out of the way in time as it embedded itself in the dirt. He kept staring at the soldier as the would-be bandit paled, becoming an ashen gray.

Renard saw the life being drained out of him, and as with the trader back in Geertstown, it seemed far faster than it should have been, certainly faster than it was happening with Renard. He saw the man's hair bleach, his skin wrinkle and crack as his hands formed into claws around the amulet. He gasped a ragged breath, and then he fell, his eyes staring at Renard in terror as he died.

"Sorcery!" one of the others cried out, as Renard started to haul himself to his feet. "He's some kind of sorcerer! All that stuff about the Hidden, and going to see the king's sorcerer... it's because he's one of them."

The two stared at Renard as he stood, and Renard stared back, trying to remember the sheer, terrifying emptiness that Void of the Hidden managed when he looked at people, or the hateful chaos of Wrath, or the deep, maddening need of Verdant. Carefully, deliberately, he lifted a finger to point it toward the men.

They ran, screaming.

Renard laughed to himself as he recovered his coin pouch and his blade. He stared down at the amulet, trying to decide if he should abandon it this time, just leave it in the woods and hope that no one would find it.

He knew that he couldn't, for all the same reasons as before. The Hidden were the biggest; they would be following, and if they got the amulet, who knew what havoc they might cause. No, for once in his life, Renard was going to do the right thing.

He took up the amulet again, feeling the slow drain begin once more. Renard set out along the woodland path, still heading for Royalsport. It couldn't be far now.

He made it perhaps half a league before his legs gave way. Renard tried to force his way back to his feet, tried to make himself move through sheer effort of will. His body seemed to have other ideas though. He lay there, collapsed on the trail, staring up at the sky. After all he'd been through with dragons and the Hidden, *this* was going to be how his life ended? On a woodland trail, close enough to his goal to reach out and touch it?

All kinds of emotions ran through Renard then, from fear of what was happening, to anger that the world could work this way, and this could happen to *him*. He didn't want to die here, like this, in a death no one would ever know, yet it seemed that he didn't get a choice.

Renard was going to die here, in a boring death that didn't even include dragons. It seemed utterly unfair, and at the same time, utterly consistent with the way his life had gone to date. His hand reached down to his belt, taking out the amulet and holding it as if he might throw it from him. Not that it would make much of a difference.

Instead, he stared at it, just stared, until his eyes fluttered closed.

CHAPTER TWENTY FOUR

Anders Samis was angry as he made his way south toward Royalsport. Angry that he'd spend so much time on a quest that had turned out to be for nothing, angry that he'd lost friends on a fool's errand, angry that his whole life had been spent leading up to something that had turned out to be a lie.

He stalked down the roads, his fur-lined cloak wrapped up in his pack, the deep blue of his other clothes enough as he walked the long route that would take him to find the sorcerer who had tricked him. The charms woven into his close-hacked blond hair jangled as he moved, providing a background note to his journey.

How had it come to this? It was supposed to be simple. He was supposed to find the fragments of the unfinished sword, to fulfill the destiny that Master Grey had set out. He was supposed to forge them together, and use them in some war that he didn't even understand. He'd been trained from birth for this, in combat and magic and more. He'd gone to all the places the fragments were supposed to be.

In every one, he'd found nothing but empty spaces.

So now he was headed to Royalsport, to demand answers. And if he didn't get those answers, he was going to put a blade through the sorcerer's heart.

He headed down the road that led south, knowing that it would take time to get there. He'd run out of horses, supplies, friends. All he had was the need for vengeance. That fueled his march south, letting him keep walking long past the point when most people would have stopped.

Occasionally, he saw soldiers in the distance, in the colors of the Southern Kingdom. Anders frowned at what that might mean, but for him, any soldier was suspect right then. Any might have been sent by the sorcerer, and after what had happened, Anders didn't know what they might try to do.

That was why, when he saw the soldier moving north along the road, Anders waited by the side, out of sight among a cluster of rocks. He didn't *look* like a soldier, of course. He wore no uniform, carried no insignia to mark him out as belonging to one side or the other, but Anders knew fighting men by the way that they moved, and this one carried a sword by his side as if he'd spent a long time readying himself to use it.

Anders waited by the roadside, waited for him to pass in silence. He had no quarrel with this man, no reason to hurt him. He held his breath as the soldier got closer, just a stride away now. Anders took an involuntary breath, and cursed himself for doing it.

The man stopped, starting to turn, and Anders knew that he'd blown his chance for this to end peacefully. He didn't hesitate, didn't even take the time to draw his sword, but leapt instead.

He slammed into the soldier, even as the other man struggled to grab his blade's grip. Anders had been trained to fight in close, as he had been trained to do so many other things, and he was both bigger and stronger than the soldier was. He struck out with a knee, then an elbow, before throwing the man to the ground.

"Who are you?" he demanded, drawing his blade.

"I'm no one," the soldier insisted.

"Don't lie to me," Anders shot back. "I've had too many people do that to me recently, including a sorcerer."

The soldier froze in place. "Wait, a sorcerer? Do you mean the *king's* sorcerer?"

Anders backed off slightly. "I'm talking about Master Grey, yes."

Just the mention of the sorcerer's name made anger rise in Anders. "If you want to live, tell me that you have nothing to do with him."

"I'm just a messenger," the man said, raising his hands and taking a step away from Anders. "Princess Lenore sent me ..."

"Sent you for what?" Anders demanded. He had heard of Princess Lenore. She was said to be beautiful, and elegant, refined and thoughtful. "Why would she send you?"

"To find the boy the sorcerer sent out," the soldier said. "I'm to give him a message."

Anders stared at him, raising his sword very slightly. "Is this a joke?"

"No joke," the soldier said. "I'm trying to find him. I have a message for him here."

"Then give it to me," Anders said. He held out his hand.

"But the message is for—"

"*I'm* the one Master Grey sent!" Anders snapped.

The messenger only looked puzzled. "No you aren't."

Anders held back the urge to strike out at the man only with difficulty. "I think I know who I am," he said. "Master Grey sent me to find the fragments of the unfinished sword. Give me the message."

"The boy Master Grey sent was called Devin," the soldier insisted. He drew his sword.

"I think I know what my name is," Anders said. "Give me the message."

"No," the soldier said. "It obviously isn't meant for you."

"Give me the message," Anders repeated. He had to know what that message said now, had to know what was going on.

"I was sent to take this message to its intended recipient, and no one else," the soldier said.

Anders started to summon magic to back up his blade. Used well, it might be able to influence this. At the very least, he might scare this man into submission. "Think carefully about what you're doing," he said. "I *will* have that message. I will know what is going on here."

"You will not," the soldier said, and then he did the one thing Anders had hoped he wouldn't do: he lunged forward with his blade, trying to skewer Anders.

Anders stepped to the side, parrying the sword, and cutting back on instinct. He held back, because he didn't want to kill this man, but that only meant that the soldier seemed to think that he had a chance to kill Anders.

"Stop this," Anders said. "Hand over the message. I don't want to kill you."

"I don't give in to bandits," the soldier said, swinging at him in an overhand cut.

"I'm not a bandit," Anders snarled, cutting into his cut, binding up with the soldier's blade and then kicking him back. "I'm the one Master Grey chose."

"I don't know who you are," the soldier said, "but you'll never be that."

He struck at Anders then and the worst part about it was that he was fast; fast enough to be dangerous; fast enough that Anders reacted with all the speed and violence of his training. Anders beat aside the incoming blade, and, before the soldier could even start to recover, he impaled the man on the tip of his arming sword.

He heard the soldier gasp as the weapon went into him. Anders had heard that sound too many times now from his friends, surprised by the things that had killed them, shocked that they could actually die, that the world could end so badly for them. He heard the clatter as the messenger's sword fell to the ground, felt the weight of the body on the end of his own blade increase as the man collapsed.

"I'm sorry," Anders said, as his foe died. "I wish this could have been different."

He felt a note of guilt as he shut the messenger's eyes, but it was nowhere near as bad as the pain he'd felt when his friends had died on this fool's errand. Now there was supposed to be some *other* boy who had been sent after the fragments?

Anders searched the messenger until he found the note that he was meant to deliver, tucked away carefully in his belt. He unfolded it with shaking fingers, reading it through, reading the name Devin over and over to himself.

He sat there by the side of the road, just sat, trying to make sense of it all. Master Grey had sent another boy to perform the same task. At *least* one other boy. There was no reason why he might not have sent ten, or a hundred. No, Anders wasn't sure that his mind could deal with that possibility. It could barely deal with the idea of one other sent off about this task that had been *his* since the moment he was born, the one that he had been *trained* for. Who was this boy? Had Master Grey had him in training for this all this time?

It potentially explained one thing, though. If this other boy, this *Devin*, had been sent on the same mission and left just a little earlier...maybe *he* had the fragments of the unfinished sword? If that was the case, then this wasn't some cruel joke on Master Grey's part, at least, not entirely. It was still cruel, to send him off about a quest where the object was missing, but at least there was a kind of sense to what was happening now.

Anders looked out along the road in the direction of Royalsport, then back the way he'd come, trying to work out what he was going to do next. His plan had been to go and confront Master Grey, but this note said that he was gone, and Royalsport fallen. What did that leave? The answer seemed clear.

He'd been sent to get the fragments of the unfinished sword, and so he would go to get them. He would find this Devin, and he would get the fragments from him. He would be the one to finish the blade, because he was the one *destined* to do it. It shouldn't be too hard to find a boy who had been looking for the fragments, out in the wild places where any strangers were looked on with fear. Anders would find him, and if the boy wouldn't hand over the fragments, Anders would probably kill him.

There was only room for one boy to fulfill this destiny, and Anders was determined that it would be him.

Chapter Twenty Five

Odd walked the castle, trying to fit in, trying to listen, trying to work out what was going to come next with this regime. He had sworn himself to teach Erin and protect Lenore, but how could he do that if he didn't know what was going on?

The noble clothes he had to wear now helped with that a little, because it meant that no one looked twice at him, the way they might have in his monk's robes. Even so, he missed them. They felt like a part of who he was by this point. Odd knew the importance of putting who he was aside sometimes, though. Hadn't he done it once before?

He moved quietly around the halls, and the trick to it was not looking like he was sneaking anywhere. It was about moving with purpose along the long stretches of the castle's corridors, finding spaces to stop and admire the artwork on the walls, taking in the scenes of the old kings or the statues of long dead heroes while he stretched his hearing, listening for what he could.

Around him, there were servants moving about on the business of the castle. Most looked frightened, although that might have something to do with the soldiers who now served as guards, moving down the corridors in pairs and giving the inhabitants baleful looks.

At least they weren't trying to stop Odd from moving around the castle alone. It seemed that he could go where he wished, so long as he did so without his sword. They didn't think he was a threat, and Odd didn't know whether to smile at the success of his small effort at disguise, or be annoyed that they were treating his skills with such contempt. The *old* Odd would probably have started killing guards just to make the point that he could, but that version of him wasn't what the princesses needed right now.

He stepped out into a long gallery space lit by the light from high windows. In it, servants were taking down the pictures of the Northern Kingdom's kings, and placing the more expensive-looking art objects into sacks under the direction of a couple of men and a woman who were dressed in what looked like stolen noble clothes. It seemed that the Quiet Men's taste in disguises had gone up in the world. Or maybe they didn't *need* to disguise themselves now that their king ruled here. Odd stepped into the shadow of a bronze statue depicting a rearing horse, wondering idly which of them looked most out of place in noble garb, them or him.

He stood there, admiring the way the sculptor had managed to capture the bunching of muscles and the detail of the hide even while he made a point of listening for the slightest trace of sound. The three Quiet Men were talking softly among themselves, and at first, Odd couldn't make out any of the words. He strained to hear, but knew that wasn't the way.

He needed to still himself instead. It was something that he was starting to be able to do in the midst of battle, but Odd had never been good at doing it when just standing there. The abbot back on Leveros had always despaired of his attempts at meditation, because there had simply been too many demons from the past lurking in Odd for his mind ever to be truly quiet.

He had to do it now though, so he stood and tried to let the world flow through him, tried to be a still point in a raging river of thoughts and feelings. Instantly, all the old horrors came to him, memories of the faces of the dead threatening to overwhelm him. Odd gritted his teeth to keep from crying out at the thought of all he'd done in the past. He couldn't do this.

He had to. The princesses didn't need a berserk knight right now; they needed someone who could listen and watch. Odd thought of the state he entered when he fought now, still and in the flow of the battle. He reached for that state, pushing away the noise of the world, determined to still himself, but that wasn't what he did when he fought, was it? He didn't shut out anything. He threw himself into the sensations of the world around him.

He felt the moment when something shifted, and the world around him seemed to clear. He found that if he relaxed, he could make out the Quiet Men's words now.

"...haven't found any sign of Tomaz," the woman said.

"He should have been here," one of the men replied. There was something gravelly in his accent. "He was sent. The princess should have been dead by now."

"Is there any point in going through with it now?" the other man put in. His voice was deeper, but smoother. "There's no need to destabilize the northerners more now, and it might annoy the emperor's new ally, Finnal."

"The emperor meant for her to be taken or killed," the woman said. "It would not look good if he ordered a death and someone lived without earning his forgiveness. We will strike tonight."

"And Finnal?" the man with the deeper voice said.

"Will not care, now that his place in things is confirmed. She was only ever a steppingstone."

Odd had heard enough. On another day, if he'd had his sword to hand, he might have attacked them, might have killed them outright. He was glad Erin wasn't with him, because she might have attacked in spite of it. That wouldn't do anything to save Lenore though. Instead, he did the thing that would, and quietly stalked from the room.

He all but ran back to Lenore's chambers. She was there, sitting near a window, looking out as if longing for the outside world. Erin had her spear out and was spinning it, practicing with it in an open section of floor. On another day, Odd might have warned her about being so careless, doing it when anyone might walk in. Right then though, there were more important concerns.

"We need to get out of the castle," Odd said.

Lenore and Erin both stared at him.

"What?" Lenore said. "Why?"

"Because it's too dangerous to stay here," Odd replied.

"I know it's bad," Erin said, "but it doesn't look like they're killing anyone else. The executions are done. If we get caught running..."

Odd knew what would happen then. If they ran, and they were caught, they would be killed. The princesses did not understand though, and that... that was his fault.

"I heard Quiet Men talking," Odd said. He looked over to Lenore. "They were talking about whether they should be killing you. They plan to do it tonight."

He saw Lenore swallow. "That's...it's frightening, Odd, but that doesn't mean that they will go through with it. I don't think Ravin will want me dead. He's *said* that he wants us to watch his rule and I think he wants...me."

"He wants you dead," Odd said.

Erin put the sheath back onto her spear, so that it looked like a staff again. "You sound very certain."

"There is...something I have to tell you," he said. Both princesses frowned at that. He knew he should have told them this before, but he hadn't wanted them to know the fear of being hunted, or to know what he'd done to defend them.

"What is it, Odd?" Lenore said.

"There was a Quiet Man before. Before the invasion. I found him in the castle. I followed him. I killed him."

"And you didn't tell us?" Lenore said. "You didn't have to hide that from us, Odd. We wouldn't have thought less of you for it."

How had she seen what he was worried about so clearly? There was something about Lenore that made Odd think about her as more than just a princess to be protected. She saw the heart of things the way a leader did. She'd seen his fear that they would be disgusted by what he'd done, and disarmed it in a few words.

He looked at Erin, and saw the eagerness to hear the violence of it. That had been the other reason that he hadn't told them. He was starting to worry about the anger that bubbled under the surface of his supposed student. It reminded him too much of the way he'd been.

"He said something in the moments before I killed him," Odd said. "He said that once he'd killed me, he would go to kill you. I thought at the time that it was just a threat to distract me, but now...now I think that is what he was sent to do. And I *know* that they are coming for you tonight."

"Why didn't you tell us this before?" Erin asked.

"I thought that I had dealt with it, and then there was the threat of the invasion to deal with." Odd looked from one to the other of them. "I am sorry, but we can't stay here."

"But with you and me by Lenore's side tonight..." Erin began.

Odd shook his head, "It wouldn't be enough, not against all the Quiet Men. They would *find* a moment to strike."

"I agree," Lenore said. "We need to escape, but we need to find a way to do it without being seen, and if they're hunting me, I don't see how. We certainly can't do it at such short notice."

"We give them what they want," Odd said. "We hide in your mother's rooms, and we let them think that they've succeeded."

"A decoy?" Lenore said.

Erin didn't seem to like that idea. "I still think we should just kill them."

"And then what?" Odd said. "There would be more, and more. Worse, we would give Ravin a reason to have *us* killed, and then Lenore would not be protected."

"So we kill all of them," Erin insisted. Odd was starting to think he was justified in his worries.

"No," Lenore said. "We'll go with Odd's plan. We'll make a decoy out of my clothes and old linen, hide it in my bed."

"It's not likely to fool the Quiet Men for long," Odd said. "But maybe it will be enough, especially if they are striking from a distance."

"Erin?" Lenore said.

Erin nodded. "You take Lenore to my mother's rooms. I'll make the decoy, then join you."

"I could do that," Odd suggested.

"No, I will," Erin said. "I *want* to."

Odd could tell that she wasn't happy about the whole situation, but it was what needed to happen.

After that, they would need to find a way to get out of the castle. They could try the passageways, because their messenger had managed to get through. If those were blocked or guarded, maybe they could try disguising themselves, or even drop a rope over the walls.

Whatever it took, Odd would find a way to get the princesses out of Royalsport. He had sworn to keep Lenore safe, and there was no way that he could do it here. If they stayed, Lenore was going to die, and Odd would do anything before he allowed that to happen.

"All right," Lenore said. "We'll do it."

CHAPTER TWENTY SIX

As the evening came, Lenore went with Odd to her mother's rooms. With every step, she rehearsed the things she wanted to say, the things she hadn't said in so long. There wouldn't be any more chances to say them now, though, at least not for a long time.

Because Erin had stayed behind to start preparing the decoy, they could at least fit in with the restrictions the guards had put in place. Lenore would have liked to bring her sister with her for this, but Erin seemed oddly determined to be the one left behind. Odd was coming with her because they weren't prepared to risk the Quiet Men attacking Lenore in the halls.

"We must be careful how we do this," Odd said softly beside her. "If others hear that you're saying goodbye, it looks suspicious. It shows that we know something is going to happen. We could just find an empty room to hide in."

"I *have* to do this," Lenore said.

Lenore thought of all the people she'd lost as she walked through the castle, heading for her mother's rooms. Her father, her brother Rodry, Nerra. Greave was gone somewhere, and Lenore didn't know if he was alive or dead. Vars was…Vars wasn't her brother anymore. There were some things that Lenore couldn't forgive.

That left her mother, and she couldn't leave without at least talking to her. If that also gave her a place to hide, it was even better.

"It's your decision," Odd said.

That was one thing Lenore found strange about Odd. From what she understood, he'd been a full-fledged Knight of the Spur, one who hadn't been good at taking orders. He was older than her, and had clearly seen far more violent situations than she had. Yet he seemed happy to follow her orders, happy to pledge himself to her, when he could have sworn himself to any lord or commander.

Lenore didn't question it though. She was too grateful for that.

There were no guards on her mother's rooms, but Lenore could see some walking the halls nearby, and she ducked inside quickly, along with Odd.

The rooms within were large, and seemed larger because there were fewer people in them than usual. Normally, the rooms would have been busy with servants and maids attending to her mother, helping to conduct the business of state. Now, Aethe sat on a couch in the middle of the room. She'd looked old before, almost broken. Now, though she wasn't at preened and perfect as she had been before the invasion, she looked stronger and more poised.

An older man Lenore recognized as an earl sat near her, talking with her in low voices.

"And you'll be ready?" her mother said.

"I'll be ready," the earl promised. He was a large man with a full beard. He rose and bowed. "Vows made under the threat of death mean nothing."

He turned and left, offering Lenore a brief nod of respect as he did so.

"What was that about, Mother?" Lenore asked as the door shut behind him.

Her mother stood to greet her, taking Lenore's hands in hers. "It's safer if you do not know."

"I..." Lenore wanted to argue, wanted to insist that she be a part of whatever her mother was doing, but she realized that she couldn't insist on that when she was planning on leaving. "I needed to talk to you, Mother. And I need to be here for a while."

"You're planning on getting out of here," her mother said.

Lenore looked at her in shock. "How... how did you know?"

"It's the safest thing for you to do, Lenore," her mother said. "I've been hoping that Sir Odd here would find a way to get you out of the city since the start of the invasion happened."

Lenore found herself choking up at that. "I ... I don't know what to say."

Her mother led her to the couch she'd just been sitting on. "You don't have to say anything, Lenore. I want you to know that I have always loved you, and that everything..." She shook her head. "No, that isn't right. I was going to say that everything I have done has been for you and your sisters, but I see now that too often I thought in terms of what would be good for the family or the realm, and not about what would make each of you happiest."

She put her hand over Lenore's as they sat, holding tight.

"I should have been a better mother to you all," she said. "I thought that if the family and the kingdom were strong, you would all be safer. Now, I realize that it doesn't work like that. Violence can visit us all, no matter how hard we try to keep safe."

"It's due to visit me tonight," Lenore said. She almost laughed that she could say that without terror overwhelming her. "They...they're coming to kill me. I'm sorry. I might be putting you in danger just by being here."

"We're all in danger," her mother said. "I'm glad you chose to come here to be safe."

Lenore didn't know what to say to that. "I just wanted to say that I love you, and to say goodbye before..."

"Before you leave," her mother said. "It's all right, you can say it. Your knight, and your sister, will keep you safe. Get out of the castle, but...don't leave the city yet. Depending on what happens, you might not have to."

Lenore frowned at that, not understanding. What was her mother planning? What could she possibly do that might make a difference to any of this?

"Mother, if it's something that we can help with, let us," Lenore said.

Her mother shook her head. "This isn't something you can help with, and even if it goes right, you might be in danger. You need to be ready to leave the city quickly, no matter what happens."

"No matter what happens with what?" Lenore asked.

Still, her mother wouldn't give any sign of what she was doing. Instead, she looked deep into Lenore's eyes.

"A lot of things could happen in the next few days, Lenore," she said. "I've always tried to teach you to be the princess people expect, but I think now that I might have lost sight of one of the most important lessons."

"What's that?" Lenore asked.

"That sometimes it's important to make a stand, not just do the thing that's politic, or easy, or safe," her mother said. "That there's more to being a queen than just doing the thing that seems to be what the nobles want. I should have stood up and refused to let Nerra leave. I should have listened to you when you had fears over your marriage. I should have done a lot of things."

"I don't blame you," Lenore said. This wasn't the time for blame, not now.

"It's not about blame now," her mother said. "It's about learning from my mistakes. I've always told you that you need to do better, to be the perfect princess, but you can be so much more than that, Lenore. You have the strength to be a true queen. You have survived more than anyone could ask of you, and not run from the danger. People love you, and will listen to you. Now, you have to have the courage to say something."

"Mother, I—" Lenore began, but her mother cut her off with a hug that caught her by surprise. It was so tight that Lenore could barely breathe.

"You must promise me that you'll look after Erin," she said.

"I think it will be Erin protecting *me*," Lenore pointed out.

Her mother shook her head. "Oh, I know Erin will keep you safe from any physical danger," she said. "But you know as well as I do that she's impetuous. She won't back down from a fight. She'll charge into danger, even when the best thing to do is to step aside and strike once it's past. She needs someone to tell her what dangers are worth fighting, and when. And she needs a sister, someone to just *be* there for her."

Looking into her mother's eyes, Lenore could see that her mother was choking back tears. It was something that Lenore had never seen from her mother, except when her father had died. She'd always been so poised, so in control, and now, it seemed as though she was struggling to maintain that.

Thoughts of Erin brought one more question hot on their heels.

"Shouldn't Erin be here by now?" Lenore said to Odd.

The knight considered for a moment or two. He frowned. "She should."

Worry built up inside Lenore. The sensible thing would be to quash that worry, sit there, wait. Her sister was probably just delayed. Maybe she was having to move carefully to avoid the attention of the guards in the halls.

"She could just be taking her time," Lenore said.

"She could," Odd agreed. He didn't sound as though he believed it.

Lenore certainly didn't. Erin should be here by now, should have finished the decoy long ago. Something was wrong.

"We should wait here," Lenore said. "We should stick to the plan."

"We should," Odd agreed.

"But if Erin is in danger..." Lenore shook her head. "I can't just wait here, Odd."

Odd nodded. "I know."

Lenore didn't want to leave. She didn't want to finally say goodbye to her mother, knowing that she might have to leave in just hours, even if her mother had urged her to wait. She stood, and as her mother stood with her, she hugged her one more time.

"Goodbye, Mother," she said. "It looks like we aren't doing this the way we planned. I hope... I hope that whatever you're talking about is real, and I'll see you again soon, but if not... I love you."

"I love you too," her mother said. "And I'm proud of you. When you see Erin, tell her that I love her too."

It was agony, pulling away from her mother at last. Lenore didn't want to do it, not in the moment when she'd finally found a version of her mother who seemed to love her for who she was, not as the princess she wanted to make her.

Lenore had to force herself to turn and walk across the floor of her mother's chambers toward the door. Every step felt like an effort, because with every one, she wanted to turn back and hug her mother again. Some part of her knew though that if she did that, she would never be able to bring herself to leave.

When she reached Odd, she put her arm through his for support, and so that he could stop her from turning back. She didn't know if she would see her mother again. It was obvious that she was planning something, with her meetings with nobles, and her talk about things maybe changing. Lenore couldn't begin to imagine what was going to happen. She had to focus on what she and her sister were going to do now. Her mother was right: she had to keep Erin safe, just as Erin and Odd kept her safe.

Right now, Erin might be in danger. Someone would be, at least.

CHAPTER TWENTY SEVEN

The hardest part of it for Erin was wearing the dress. She'd done everything she could in her life to avoid wearing elegant dresses designed to make her look more like a princess. Now, when looking more like a princess was the whole *point*, it still wasn't easy.

It didn't help that the princess in question was Lenore, who was taller, more elegant, and actually *fit* the blue silk and velvet dress that Erin was currently wearing. Of course, the armor underneath made that harder, but a lot of it was down to the height difference. The hem of the dress trailed on the floor as Erin considered the best way to disguise her features.

Her hair was the big problem. They both had dark hair, but Lenore's was long and lustrous, while hers was cut boyishly short to stop anyone grabbing it in a fight. In the end, Erin found a jeweled caul that Lenore might have used to cover her hair and stuffed it with smallclothes until it looked the right shape.

She looked around, taking in the darkening interior of Lenore's room. It was more elegant and opulent than her own had ever been. Her mother had tried to make her have all the drapes and the gilded ornaments, the tapestry work and the things for painting, but Erin had preferred space in which she could move freely.

Now, the ornaments and the sewing supplies in one corner of the room gave Erin an idea. Very carefully, she moved every ornament she could find to the edge of the stand or table on which it sat. Just as carefully, she took the finest pieces of thread that she could find and started to tie them to the ornaments, stretching them out between them so that they formed a silent web of tripwires.

She took out her spear and set it under the covers of the bed. She lay down with it, curling around it to disguise the shape of it.

Erin lay in bed, still and silent. Her heart beat faster than it had since the fighting on the streets. She could feel fear tucked away inside her, but she kept it down the way she knew best: with the anger that never seemed to go away.

Some of that anger was with the Quiet Men; the idea that they might just come to murder her sister was enough to make her blood boil. At least as much of it, though, was with the idea that she wasn't supposed to do anything about it. She was supposed to run away, to let Ravin's people think they'd won. She was supposed to just *give up*.

Erin couldn't do that. She couldn't even understand how Odd had asked her to do that. He was supposed to be this mighty warrior, filled with fury and battle rage, yet in this he was backing away as meekly as ... well, as the princess Erin's mother had tried to make her be.

She lay with her eyes just slightly open, able to take in a little of the room. Erin tried to keep her breathing slow and deep, because sleeping people didn't breathe like waking ones. She put her energy into the best facsimile of sleep that she could manage, trying to play her part, even though subterfuge wasn't something she'd ever truly been good at. Even when they'd been little, and Greave had wanted them all to act out parts from plays he'd found in the castle library, Erin had never been good at pretending to be someone else. She hadn't seen the point in it.

Now, though, there *was* a point, and Erin was determined to get this right.

The hardest part was the waiting. That was probably the one advantage of Odd's plan, because a dummy could just be left there as long as it needed to be. Erin had never been good at being still, and now she was having to stay that way for so long that there was a danger she might *actually* go to sleep.

How long would she have to lie here? How did she know that the assassins were even going to show up? Wouldn't the sensible thing be for them to come in the dead of night, not during the day? Was she being stupid, lying here like this? Should she just get up? It wasn't like she could lie here forever, waiting until—

Erin thought she saw a shadow pass across the edge of her limited vision, and she closed her eyes completely for a moment or two, not wanting to risk them seeing that she was waiting. Having fought Quiet Men before, she knew they were dangerous, yet in that moment, it wasn't fear that filled her: it was anticipation.

Erin's hand tightened about the haft of her spear as she waited. She counted her breaths as they grew closer, knowing that she would have to pick her moment carefully. She heard the clatter of a gilded ornament falling as a foot snagged one of her tripwires, followed by a muffled curse.

Now!

Erin leapt up with a battle cry, and her now wide open eyes took in three figures, a woman and two men. Caught by surprise, they hesitated for just a moment, and in that moment, Erin was already acting.

She flung the covers at the man who was closest, stepped past him and struck with her spear at the woman. She gasped as the point of it buried itself in her chest, deep enough to come out of the other side. Erin wrenched it clear and hit the remaining man with the butt of her spear, even as his knife scraped off the armor hidden beneath her dress. Erin spun toward him, then cursed as her feet snagged in the stupid, too long hem. Rather than fight to keep standing, she threw herself to her knees, letting his next knife slash whisper above her head. Erin struck up with her spear, plunging it into the Quiet Man's stomach, then forcing it up into his chest.

He died, but even as he did so, he did the one thing Erin didn't expect: he grabbed for the haft of the spear, clutching it in a grip that promised never to let go. Erin yanked at it, but the spear wouldn't come out of his dying body, and already to her left, she could see the remaining killer disentangling himself from the covers Erin had thrown. He came out with a hatchet in one hand, advancing on her rapidly.

Erin let go of her spear and threw herself to one side, so that the hatchet struck nothing but air. She came up and backed away, hands spread wide. She could see one of the assassins' knives on the floor nearby, so if she could just get to it…

The hatchet man came at her too fast for that, his weapon swinging for Erin's head. Erin didn't back away, but charged forward instead, inside the path of the blow. She slammed into her foe, grappling for control of the weapon while she kicked and kneed and head butted. The Quiet Man struck back, and Erin winced as blows slammed into her ribs.

She wasn't built for grappling in close with a grown man, but now she was committed to it, and Erin wasn't going to give up. The important thing was to keep the weapon away from her foe's body, where he couldn't switch hands with it, and to keep attacking, hoping that one of her blows would do enough damage to make him drop the hatchet. Erin struck and struck, kicking into his knees, bringing knees up into his body, thighs, and groin. The Quiet Man seemed to be angry enough now to just ignore the pain.

In desperation Erin shoved herself clear of her foe, flinging herself for the knife she'd seen. She took it in a roll, and heard the hatchet clatter down on the marble of the floor as she came up with it. Erin turned, and without hesitating, she flung the knife.

It slammed into the throat of her opponent, hilt deep, and he froze in place at the impact, staring down at the weapon that had struck him. His raised hatchet fell to the floor, and he followed it, slumping limply as he died.

Erin was still on the floor staring at him when the door opened to let in Odd and Lenore.

"What have you done?" Odd said, in a shocked voice.

"What you did with the first one," Erin said. "I dealt with the situation."

"But I told you how dangerous this was. We agreed—"

"*You* agreed," Erin snapped back. "You and Lenore decided what would happen. Well, guess what? I get to make my own decisions, and I'm not going to let anyone try to kill my sister without dying for it."

"This was a stupid, dangerous thing to do," Odd said.

"I'm fine though. I wasn't hurt, and they're dead." It reminded Erin too much of the ways Commander Harr had spoken to her. Odd was supposed to be different.

"Are you all right?" Lenore asked her.

"I'm fine," Erin assured her as she stood. "I might have gotten blood on your dress."

Lenore seemed mostly concerned that she was okay. Odd still seemed angry.

"You don't realize what you've done, do you?"

"I ended the threat," Erin snapped. How could they not understand?

Odd shook his head. "You've killed *these* assassins, but there will be more, and more after that."

"So we kill them too. Besides, we're supposed to be leaving, aren't we?" Erin said.

"We might have to wait for that," Lenore said. "Mother said something. Something... might be happening."

"It isn't about when we leave," Odd said. "It's about you letting your anger get the better of you, Erin. You know that if they find the bodies, Ravin won't need to send assassins. He'll have an excuse to execute you, Erin. If they find out what happened just now, we could all die."

To Erin, it sounded like he was being dramatic. She would kill a hundred Quiet Men if she could, a thousand. She'd seen the kinds of things they did. They deserved it. She was just doing the same as Odd, trying to protect her sister, trying to make all of this right.

"We need to clear all this up," Odd said. "You think you saved your sister today? You might just have condemned all of us."

CHAPTER TWENTY EIGHT

The moment the boat touched the shoreline, Aurelle leapt from it. She felt better the moment her feet touched the ground; she was done with traveling by boat. Looking round, she could see that the sailors left behind her were almost as relieved as she was, clearly glad to be rid of her.

Almost as soon as she was ashore, those sailors used poles to push their vessel away. Aurelle watched them go for a moment, but only to make sure that they weren't going to double back and attack her. Then she set off in the direction where she believed Royalsport lay, hurrying forward.

It wouldn't take her long now that she was on dry land again. Woodland lay in between, and there were always dangers in that in times like this, but Aurelle was confident. Any bandit stupid enough to attack her would quickly learn the price of doing so.

Aurelle sighed at that thought. She knew what Greave would think of it; it was exactly the kind of bloodthirstiness that he would hate. On the other hand, *he* wasn't the one having to walk through potentially bandit-infested woodland alone, and given what she was planning to do at the end of this, worrying about who she killed on the way seemed a little pointless.

She plunged into the woods, and for the first little way, it was hard getting used to being on land again. She kept walking, though, because she wasn't going to let anything get in between her and the men she had to kill in Royalsport.

Things were so different as she walked from the way they'd been on the boat. Even small things, like the difference in the light beneath the canopy, were different. There hadn't been the sound of birdsong out on the ocean, except for the gulls. There hadn't been the scents of flowers opening...

...or the strange, twisted dead figure on the floor.

Instantly, Aurelle was on alert, a knife in her hand. The man was dressed like some kind of soldier or bandit, but he looked old and twisted, his flesh papery. Aurelle reached out to touch him, and that flesh fell away like ash, so devoid of any life now that it blew away almost to nothing. What had happened here?

Aurelle didn't know, but she moved forward cautiously, a dagger palmed in her hand. She kept moving along the trail, trying to keep her eyes open for the slightest sign of danger.

When she saw the second body, she almost walked past without stopping. There was something about this man though that made her stop. He didn't look the same as the bandit before, even though his skin and his hair were bleached out in the same way, as if the life had been sucked out of him. He looked like he had once been a big, vibrant, red-haired man. He'd probably been good looking, before this. Now, it looked as though he was just an empty, ashen shell.

She was still staring at him when she realized that his chest was rising and falling, however slowly.

Before all this, she might have moved on anyway. This was none of her business, and everything about it said to Aurelle that getting involved would only mean trouble. Now though, she could all too easily imagine what Greave's expression would be if she just walked away. With a sigh, she started toward the man.

His eyes snapped open as she approached.

Reflex made Aurelle press her knife to his throat, because she was still half-convinced that this was all some kind of trap.

"If you turn out to be a bandit," she said, "this is going to be a very bad day for both of us."

Renard stared up at the woman standing over him, pressing a knife to his throat in a suspiciously expert manner. He had to admit that, if he was going to have his throat cut by anyone, she was a particularly beautiful choice for it. Her hair was a red to match his, her features sharply defined, her eyes a piercing green. She was wearing gray traveling clothes, and the blood on them suggested to Renard that it wouldn't be a good idea to move suddenly right then.

"I'm not...a bandit," Renard managed.

"You're something though, aren't you?" the woman said. "You think I don't know a dishonest man when I meet one?"

Renard tried his most winning smile. "Dishonest, me?"

She increased the pressure of the knife just a fraction. To be fair, she wasn't the first woman who had done that.

"Well, I *have* been a notorious thief," Renard admitted. "I've swindled, and stolen, and broken into impossible places. I even managed to take gold from Lord Carrick's vaults. My name's Renard."

"I've never heard of you," the woman said, but he noted the faintest beginnings of a smile on the edges of her lips.

"I'm...faintly insulted," Renard said. "Also, this is normally the point at which you tell me who you are."

The woman seemed to consider that.

"I'm Aurelle," she said.

"And what manner of scoundrel are you?" Renard asked her. Talking to her, he felt a little stronger. "And before you say that you aren't one, I should point out that I know dishonest folk too."

"I'm..." Renard waited, not sure that she would answer. "...I guess you could say that I'm a spy. And a killer. Or I was supposed to be."

Renard looked her over and took a guess.

"You're with the House of Sighs?" he asked.

She froze in place. "You do realize that you just called me a whore?"

"That's not what I said at all," Renard said. "Come on, we can both pretend that's all the House of Sighs is, but among the right people, it's hardly a secret."

Maybe he was overstepping, saying that. It probably wasn't a good idea to play at being clever when there was a killer in front of him. On the other hand, if he was dying anyway, it wasn't as if he exactly had much to lose.

"All right," Aurelle said. "I work for the House. You realize that I should cut your throat just for working that out?"

Renard would have shrugged, but he didn't want to risk that much movement, right then. "I think if you were going to do that, you'd have done it already. Besides, I've looked into the eyes of people who are truly cruel, truly evil. I don't think you're one of them."

"You might be surprised," Aurelle said, but she still took the knife away from Renard's throat. She sat opposite him, staring at him. "What are you doing out here? Why are you like this? Why was there a man further back who went into dust the moment I touched him?"

"Ah," Renard said. "He tried to rob me, and fell victim to my deadly, sorcerous powers."

Almost as soon as he said it, he regretted it, because Aurelle stood up and started to walk away.

"Wait!" Renard called out.

"Why should I, if you're going to lie to me?" she shot back, glancing over her shoulder. "Why shouldn't I just abandon you?"

"All right," Renard said. "But the truth isn't going to sound much more believable."

"Let me be the judge of that," Aurelle said.

"The man back there *was* one of three who tried to rob me, but one of the things he tried to steal is dangerous, an amulet."

"What amulet?" Aurelle asked.

Renard managed to find the strength to take it out, holding it up for her to see. She went to touch it, and Renard jerked it back.

"I wouldn't," he said. "The bandit only took it for a few seconds."

"So why are you able to hold it?" she asked.

Renard shook his head. "I don't know. It's still draining me ..."

"Obviously."

"... but slower."

"Why not throw it away?" Aurelle asked. "Why not leave it in the hand of the bandit who took it and run?"

Renard laughed. "You think I didn't try? I sold it to a fence, and he died, and ... the Hidden are searching for it."

"The Hidden?" Aurelle said. "I thought they were a story."

"They aren't," Renard assured her. "They're terrifying beyond anything I've known. They're the ones who sent me to find the amulet for them in the first place, after I got caught stealing from Lord Carrick."

"I thought you said that you succeeded in that," Aurelle asked.

"I did, but then there was an inn, and a woman and..."

Renard heard her laugh then. "Of course there was. But if the Hidden want this amulet so badly, isn't that just one more reason to abandon it and run?"

"It's...too dangerous for them to have," Renard. "Too much power. This amulet...I think it's something to do with dragons."

"There aren't any dragons in the Northern Kingdom anymore," Aurelle said.

"Tell that to the one who chased me out of the place where I found this," Renard replied. "Or the one who burnt Geertstown while I was in it. They seem to be attracted to it."

"So you're being chased by the Hidden and by random dragons?" Aurelle asked.

"Trying to get to Royalsport to see the sorcerer there, to see if he'll help," Renard said. He sighed. "Doing the right thing is a lot harder than I thought it would be."

Aurelle looked out into space for a while. "Yes, it is."

"What's your story?" Renard asked.

"I was sent to kill a good man," she said. "I ended up trying to protect him, but he died anyway. Now, I'm going to kill the men who ordered it."

She seemed to think for a while then walked away.

"Wait!" Renard shouted after her. "You're just going to abandon me, after all of this?"

He tried to stand, but didn't have the strength. He started to crawl in the direction she'd gone.

He was still doing it when she came back with a stout-looking branch, and Renard could only feel embarrassed as she helped him to his feet, shoving the branch under one of his arms to lean on.

"Come on," she said. "We've still got a way to go if we're going to get to Royalsport before you keel over."

CHAPTER TWENTY NINE

Nerra sat astride Shadr as hordes of the animalistic Lesser gathered on Sarras's coast. She watched them in awe, simply because of their numbers, but there were better things on the beaches to look at that way.

The dragons perched there as Shadr did, each with its spot on the sand. There might have been a hundred of them, spread out there, yet none flew, because Shadr did not wish them to fly until the moment came. Nerra could only wonder at the power that could command so many.

Our power, my Nerra, Shadr sent into her mind, *You and I together. The moment the queen of dragons found her Perfected, the moment became right for this.*

Nerra could see others of the Perfected there with dragons, standing by them or already perched atop them. Not all of them were bonded to the creatures, though; some moved among the Lesser to marshal the beast-like versions of their kind, while others dragged great boats, raft-like and built from jungle wood, into the water. Nerra couldn't see how they might be propelled, until one of the dragons, a smaller yellow one with an orange edge to some of its scales, waded into the water to take hold of a thick cable of jungle vines in its teeth.

Not all of the boats were built by her kind. Some were clearly vessels of the Southern Kingdom, taken in the slaughter that had befallen their colonies, or captured as they sailed too close to Sarras. There had always been stories of boats going missing if they tried to reach the third landmass of the Three Kingdoms; now, Nerra knew one of the reasons why.

The numbers were strange in a way, with many, many of the Lesser ones, fewer of the Perfected, and fewer still of them bonded to dragons.

The dragons were the fewest of all, yet each one of them was an island around which all the rest of the activity took place. The Perfected did as they commanded, and the Lesser were herded by the Perfected onto the waiting boats.

It is time, Shadr sent out, and the echoes of that thought seemed to carry across the beach. *Hold on, Nerra.*

She spread her wings, and Nerra clung to the scales of her neck as all the dragons of the beach took flight in unison. Nerra felt the power of Shadr's bunching muscles beneath her as the dragon burst into the sky, the ground quickly giving way to the ocean below.

Behind and below Nerra, the ships started to move, shifting out into the deep water, pulled by the dragons. They were dark with the mass of the Lesser who swarmed on them, and Nerra was glad that she wasn't one of those Perfected who had to be down there among them, trying to control the chaos.

You will have your own task when we reach our destination, Shadr sent to her. Nerra could see that destination rising quickly in the distance, so small in comparison to the continent it nestled against.

The Isle of Hope sat there, and on it, those who had cast her out.

"Tell me what I need to do," Nerra said. The wind ripped her words away, but Shadr heard them, nonetheless. The dragon told her, told her all that she would need to say when they landed, the choice that she would have to give those there.

The wingbeats of the assembled dragons devoured the distance between the mainland and the Isle of Hope, making the journey far quicker than Nerra had on her tiny boat. Even the boats with them moved quickly, dragged along by those dragons who had been given the task by Shadr, or piloted by those of the Perfected who knew about such things from their previous lives.

The island came into focus as it grew closer, its single volcano looking so small compared to those of Sarras, its trees less lush. The village at its heart sat there as Nerra had left it, those with the dragon sickness moving about their business between the low, squat buildings.

Except that Nerra could see now that it wasn't a sickness, it was a blessing.

Shadr swooped low over the island, while the other dragons circled. Nerra could hear the cries of fear now as people ran for cover, some shutting themselves in houses, others running for the foliage beyond the village.

The dragon's wings spread to slow her as she landed in the middle of it all, touching down in a cloud of dust in the village square. People were still running, and Nerra slid down from Shadr's back, watching them. She knew that she should feel sympathy, the desire to help them, fear on their behalf. Instead, she found herself thinking of the looks of fear they had turned her way before, the hatred on some of their faces as she had returned to the village.

She could feel the anger that bubbled beneath the surface in her, and the contempt for things that were still human, when they had the chance to be so much more. Another, smaller part said that those feelings weren't right somehow, but Nerra couldn't understand how they would be anything *but* right.

She started to speak, but a flicker of thought from Shadr stopped her. *Wait.*

Nerra waited, watching, and another flicker of command from the dragon went out, this time to those circling. They plunged down, their mouths opening wide, and Nerra heard the dull roar as white-hot flames poured out.

The roofs of the houses beneath didn't stand a chance, lighting one by one like candles touched by a taper. Flames burst into the air in response to the ones that swept over them, and the inhabitants ran screaming from them.

One of the dragons dropped down on the building that held the twisted ones, the ones just a day or two from Kleos's knife. It whipped a tail that was as long as the building was wide, and a hole smashed in the wall, letting the monstrous forms pour free.

No, Nerra realized, not monstrous; merely those of the Lesser. They came out snarling and raging, and Nerra stepped to them.

"Stop," she told them, and they stopped. The others there, the ones who still looked like the human-things, the ones who were still as she had been, stood and stared at her too.

"The world is changing," Nerra said, as Shadr had told her. "The false world of humans is coming to an end. The reign of dragons will return to it, and the humans will be given the choice to serve or to die."

"That doesn't sound like much of a choice for us!" one of the women there shouted.

Nerra looked over at her with kindness. She still didn't understand.

"*You* are not human," she said. "The so-called sickness you have is not a sickness, but a process of transformation into what you were always meant to be. The humans cursed the transforming waters, but I survived them, and I became Perfected. With our help, you can be too."

"What if we don't want to?" a man said from near the back. He gestured to the flames consuming the buildings. "Do you burn us?"

Nerra put a hand on Shadr's flank, feeling the bulk and the warmth of her there, towering above the people watching, and even the buildings.

"If you wish to be human, you will have the humans' choice," Nerra said. "You can serve as they will until such time as the transformation claims you. Then you will turn into one of the Lesser."

She gestured to the ones who had broken free with the sweep of the dragon's tail.

"Or you can be more," she said. "So *much* more. The world can be remade, with you at its heart, serving the species that is truly strongest."

"You call that more?" a figure demanded, pushing his way through the crowds. He was older and bearded, dressed in the robes of those meant to take care of the island. He had his dagger in his hand, as if even now, he might be able to use it to kill Nerra. "I wish I'd killed you when I had a chance."

"Hello, Kleos," Nerra said, keeping her voice level. "I was wondering where you were. Let's not pretend that you *wouldn't* have killed me if you could. The only reason you sent me to Sarras was because you knew I could finish you easily."

"I should have tried anyway," Kleos snapped back. "All my life, that has been my task: to stop this from coming, by stopping things like you from coming into being."

"And you have failed," Nerra said. "You, of course, will not have the chance to change. You have never been what we are. Is that why you've always tried to kill us? Because you're jealous of what we can become?"

"I kill you because you're monsters. Humans have defeated your kind before, and they will again."

Nerra shook her head. It wouldn't happen like that. With Shadr by her side, it was so obvious that it wouldn't.

"The world will be ours again," Nerra said. She could feel her anger at him, and at everything he'd tried to do, hardening into something more dangerous. It was hard, right then, to work out which parts of that were her and which were Shadr. "The only question is what place in it people choose to have."

"I want no part of any world your kind create," Kleos snapped at her.

Nerra paused for a moment, hearing Shadr's response before she said it. "You weren't being offered one."

The dragon reared up, opening her mouth so wide that she could have swallowed a sheep or a horse in a single gulp. The shadows she'd breathed before poured out from her, but these were shadowed flames, and Kleos screamed as they touched him. They seemed to be so cold that they burned, enervating what they touched, drawing out life as they struck, until a withered corpse struck the ground.

Nerra felt the moment when Shadr switched to true flames, incinerating that body, turning it to ash. In seconds, there was nothing left but a darkened patch on the ground. She could see the others there looking at it with horror, but not all of them. Some looked on with awe, and those were the ones Nerra knew would drink the waters, become Perfected.

They would travel with them, and the rest of the world would be offered its choice: join them or burn.

Chapter Thirty

Greave knelt over the campfire he had created, watching the half gourd in which he was boiling ingredients. His concentration was total, watching the colors of the mixture, and the flame.

The slightest shift, and he lifted the gourd, pouring the mixture into cooling seawater, watching it form a perfect sphere. He lifted it with two sticks, because this wasn't something to touch with bare skin, and then plunged it into a waiting mixture, where it started to dissolve with a hissing sound.

"It's working. It's actually working," Greave muttered to himself. He found that talking as he did it helped. He would have liked someone to talk to, would have liked *Aurelle* there to talk to, but that wasn't an option anymore. He had only the deserted space of the island, and the ocean beyond.

How long had he been here now? Greave had lost track. Days, probably. Long enough that the straggles of his dark beard had grown into something thicker, and his hair was tangled with sea salt.

He'd survived by focusing on what needed to be done. First, he'd focused on the things he needed to survive, and he'd found them. Then, he'd focused on the components he needed for the cure, and to his shock, he'd found *them* as well. At least, most of them, more than he could have hoped for given that he was out in the wilds.

It was amazing how much he'd been able to do with so little in the way of resources. He'd found ways to approximate processes he'd only read about in books, things he'd been sure that could only be performed with the full equipment of the House of Scholars.

Now, he had something that was only a couple of steps away from being able to help his sister, if he could find her, if he could get it to her. The thought of actually being able to help Nerra made Greave's heart swell with satisfaction, and with hope. He'd traveled so far, been through so much, for this, and now he'd achieved it. He *had* a cure, or at least most of it. He poured it into a water bottle and stoppered it.

He only wished that his attempts at boat building were going as well. Oh, a raft was easy enough, but Greave had already seen how little control that gave in the face of the open sea. He would need far more, and he wasn't sure that he had the skills to do anything about it.

Still, he was trying. His efforts were currently up on two logs, split timber and twine joining together in something that still looked too far away from what he wanted. In some ways, it was made harder because Greave at least understood the theory of it; he'd read books about the design of ships, from ancient galleys right up to barges that might try to brave the rushing power of the Slate. It just made it clear all the ways that his efforts fell short.

Greave was still trying to work out the best way to shape a keel when he saw a dot on the horizon, out on the ocean to the southwest. At first, Greave thought that it must be a mistake, a trick of the light designed to deceive him.

Then the shape resolved itself, and Greave saw a boat approaching. It was a strange little thing, twin hulled and dart-like, with a single triangular sail that seemed to be able to bring it in against the breeze. Greave found himself reminded of Lenari's *On the properties of bodies in air*, and strange diagrams of birds' wings. Then he realized that he didn't have enough time to think about that, because if he wasn't careful, his one chance for rescue was going to pass him by.

Greave rushed back to his campfire, grabbing a burning branch with either hand. Lifting them, he waved them back and forth above his head, determined to attract attention if he could.

The worst part was that there was no way of knowing what was happening, if the pilot of the boat had even seen him. Yet slowly, it seemed that the boat *was* growing closer, was heading in the direction of the island.

Greave kept waving as it got closer, watched as it came right up to the beach and the figure of a man leapt off it, starting to drag it up onto the sand. Greave went to help, and found himself alongside a small, wiry man with the tattoos of a sailor across weathered skin.

"I'm Bodrin," the man said, as they pulled the small vessel up above the tideline.

"Greave."

The man frowned. "The only man I know of that name's the prince."

Greave wasn't sure what to say to that. The newcomer seemed friendly enough, but Greave was cautious. If he'd learned anything from Aurelle, it was that people weren't always what they seemed.

"I was...named for him," Greave lied. Aurelle had taught him about that, too.

"Wasn't expecting to find anyone out here," Bodrin said. He sat down on the sand near Greave's fire. Greave sat down a little way away from him.

"I didn't mean to be here," Greave said. "My raft got washed here, and then I had no way back."

The other man looked at him with sympathy. "That's hard. Where are you from?"

"Royalsport," Greave said.

"Then maybe you're better off out here," Bodrin said. "Things are pretty bad in the kingdom since the king died."

"Since my...the king is dead?" Greave said. Emotions rushed through him at those words, more than he'd thought would be there given what a disappointment he'd always been to his father. "How? What's been happening?"

"Godwin the Third was killed, they say murdered, and Prince Rodry died trying to save Princess Lenore from the southerners after they kidnapped her."

"Rodry's dead as well?" Greave said, and he couldn't keep the shock out of his voice. "And Lenore was...was *taken*?"

The shock, anguish, and grief rolled over him in waves. He'd missed so much. He'd missed things that *mattered,* and that hurt more than he could find words for. He felt tears roll down his cheeks, the kind of tears his father would have chided him for as being too effeminate.

Bodrin stared at him. "You're not just named for the prince, are you?"

"I..." Greave thought about lying, but the truth was that he was no good at it. He wasn't Aurelle. "No, I'm not. I'm Prince Greave."

"Then what are you doing out here?" the other man asked.

"I went looking for a way to help my sister by finding a cure for the scale sickness," Greave said. "I went to Astare to find it, and when the southerners came there, I escaped on a raft. I was washed here, and I've been stuck here ever since."

"*I* just got out when the fighting came," Bodrin said. "It sounds like, even if you did it by accident, you got out at the right time too. With Royalsport falling to King Ravin's men—"

"Wait. What?" Greave demanded. That was another shock, as bad as the rest but worse. That his father and his brother were dead sent grief bursting in his heart, but the thought of Royalsport falling did worse than that: it made him afraid. All that remained of his family was in Royalsport. By now, *Aurelle* would be in Royalsport.

"I need to get back there," Greave said.

"Back *there?*" Bodrin replied. "Are you stupid? There's nothing waiting there but death."

"Everyone I care about is there," Greave said. Apart from Nerra, it was true. Greave didn't know *where* she was right now. Finding her had been the next part of what he was going to do. Now, even that seemed secondary.

"Then everyone you care about is dead," Bodrin said. "Sorry, I know that sounds harsh, but there's nothing you can do. You're better off here. Looks like you have things set up well here. We wait, we ride out the storm, and when things are back to normal, we—"

It seemed that Greave had learned *one* thing from Aurelle. He lunged forward, drawing a knife, and pressing it to the sailor's throat.

"I need you to take me to Royalsport, right now," he said.

"You won't kill me," Bodrin said. "From what I've heard about Prince Greave, you're not tough like your brother Rodry, or cruel like Vars. Even your sister Erin is—"

Greave moved the knife and cut a thin line across his cheek.

"Damn it!"

"A month ago, and you'd have been right," Greave said. "But in that time, I've lost a sister I cared about and the woman I loved. My father and my brother are dead, and now all the rest are in danger. You don't *know* what I will and won't do. The truth is that neither do I." He shook his head. "That's not true. I know one thing I *am* going to do: I'm going to Royalsport. I'm going to take your boat to do it."

"You'd die out on the ocean before you even got there," Bodrin said. "You don't know which way to go, and you don't know how to make a boat live through the waves."

"If I have to, I'll risk it," Greave replied, "but I'm hoping you'll take me. Look, I'm sorry about your cheek, but I have to get back. Even if it means my death, I have to find out what's happening to my family."

"And you just expect me to help you?" Bodrin said.

"Hasn't there ever been anyone you've cared for?" Greave asked. "Anyone you'd do anything for? Please, you don't have to risk anything; you don't even have to get close to the city, just drop me on the coast so that I can walk. Do that, and you can disappear back here until it's all done. I have some coin. If I die, you're better off by that much. If by some miracle I live through all this though...then you'll be owed a favor by a prince. You've nothing to lose, and maybe everything to gain."

"I..." The sailor hesitated.

"Please," Greave said.

He nodded, and even if he didn't look certain about it, it was good enough for Greave. "I'll do it."

"Thank you," Greave said.

"Don't thank me. I'm probably taking you to your death."

Greave knew that, but at the same time, he knew that he had to get to Royalsport. He had to find a way to help, even if it cost him everything. It was time to go home.

CHAPTER THIRTY ONE

Orianne crouched in the darkness of the basement where Finnal's thugs had left her, fear and hunger vying for control over her, even though she wasn't in a position to do anything about either one. That only made it worse, in a lot of ways.

There was pain, too, from the bruises where they'd struck her, trying to learn what she knew about Finnal, and then what secrets she had of Lenore's. Her dark hair was in disarray, and caked with sweat, while the finery of her clothes had tears and stains from where they'd thrown her in here.

They'd asked her questions, over and over again. Orianne had spun them lies and half-truths, knowing that it was better than saying nothing, but not willing to betray her friend. Lenore would come for her.

Eventually.

Orianne tried not to give in to despair at that thought. She didn't know how long she'd been down here now, hidden away, kept only because they'd decided that she might be useful. She didn't know if Lenore would ever find her, and only had faith to say that she would be coming at all.

Orianne sat there with her fears until a chink of light showed above her where the door was, and that just brought with it a different kind of fear. When a pair of Finnal's manservants approached through the doorway, that fear only increased.

"Looks like we're going on a journey," one of them said. He had a rasping voice, and a dangerous glint in his eyes. He grabbed Orianne's hands, binding them before her.

"Where to?" she asked, even though she knew asking would do nothing good for her.

"Somewhere they won't find your body," the other one said. His voice was smoother, and he actually smiled as he pulled a dark hood down over her head.

They made her walk then, and Orianne felt the sensation of steps under her feet. She tried to throw herself clear of the men in desperation, but they just grabbed her and held her, laughing as they did it.

"I am nobly born," Orianne said through the cloth of the hood, as if that made a difference. It did to some, though, and she would say anything right then if it would help. "And the princess is my friend. Kill me, and—"

One of them struck her; she couldn't tell which one, only feel the pain of it.

"Why do you think we're taking you somewhere you won't be found?" the one with the honeyed voice said.

They made her walk then. When Orianne refused to, they dragged her, so it was simply easier to go along, even though she knew what waited at the end of all this. She mounted another step and was pushed into a seat. The rumble of wheels on cobbles followed, along with the sensation of movement.

Whatever carriage or cart she was in halted briefly, and Orianne had the hope that maybe guards had found her, or people sent by Lenore. Maybe her sister was waiting to pounce, even now.

"What's this then?" a voice asked, in an accent that it took Orianne a moment to place as being from the Southern Kingdom.

"Someone who needs to be disposed of," the man with the rasping voice said, and that shocked her, that he could just talk about it so openly.

"Then why not cut her throat and be done with it?" the voice beyond the carriage asked.

"Because that's not what Lord Finnal wants."

Orianne knew she had to try to save herself, had to try *something*. "Please," she called out. "I serve Princess Lenore. Please *help* me."

That just earned her another blow that made her head ring. Certainly, it didn't bring the rescue that she'd been hoping for.

"All right," the man said. "Do what you want."

"Oh, we will," the one with the smoother voice said, in a tone that made a shiver run down Orianne's spine.

The carriage, or wagon, or whatever it was rumbled back into motion.

"A lot of things have changed since you got yourself caught," the one with the rasping voice said. "You've been sitting safe in the dark while the southerners took the kingdom. Emperor Ravin rules here now, and your precious princess... by now, she's probably dead."

"No!" Orianne exclaimed, half lunging out of her seat. Rough hands pushed her back into place.

"Why do you think you're being disposed of?" the other one said. "You were useful as long as the princess was alive. But Ravin wanted her dead for denying him, and Finnal's father decided it was better to switch sides for now, so she's dead, and soon, you will be too."

The worst part was that he said it like it was a simple fact; just a chore to be taken care of. Orianne tried to think of something she could say, something she could do, that might change that fact. The worst part was that she couldn't think of a single thing that might help. All she could do was sit there and wait for the moment when they would kill her.

The carriage stopped far too soon, and they shoved her from it hard enough that Orianne stumbled, then fell. One of them shoved her forward, then yanked the hood from her head.

Orianne blinked in the sunlight. She was in a clearing, just a little way from the road, surrounded by trees. She was half-blind right then and terrified, but even so, she knew that a blade could be coming for her any moment. All her instincts said that she should cower and blink, but that was the way that she would die. She got her feet under her and she ran.

Hands grabbed for her, but she brushed clear of them and plunged into the trees. She heard the men running after her, but Orianne didn't look back. She kept her eyes on the brush of the forest floor, feet crunching over it, breaking branches as she ran.

Even that wasn't enough, though. Her foot snagged on a root, and then she was tumbling, plunging face first into the leaf litter, her bound hands not able to stop her.

She rolled to her back, and the men were coming for her. Now that she was out of the dark, she could see them better, not that there was much about them that she wanted to look at. They were both of average height, one with a square face and close-cropped hair, one with a short beard and a lean frame. She'd only seen them as shadows in the dark before now, but her focus was on the blades in their hands.

"Here's as good as anywhere," the lean one said. "This far from the road, we can take our time."

"Please," Orianne begged, even as she tried to work out if she could run again, but there was no way that she could get up and get clear before they were on her. "Please, you don't need to do this."

"I *want* to do this," the other one said.

"And a job's a job," the lean one added. He ran a thumb along the edge of his blade. He took a step forward.

Orianne was terrified in that moment, certain that she was about to die, and knowing that with men like these, it would happen in the worst ways possible. Then something made her frown. She thought that she saw a flicker of movement in the trees, somewhere behind them.

It was all Orianne could do to keep her eyes on the men in front of her; to not call out for help, or draw attention to that flicker, even as the square-featured one brought his knife close to her, taunting her with it, and all the ways he might hurt her with it. Orianne didn't have to feign the tremble of fear that ran through her at its touch, but she *did* have to force herself to be still as two figures padded from the trees behind the men: a man and a woman, the former looking old before his time as he leaned on a crude crutch, the later red-haired and beautiful, looking strangely familiar...

The moment when they struck was as sudden as it was brutal; the kind of execution the two men had come to the woods for, even if they'd thought they'd be the ones doing it. The woman stepped up behind the square-featured man and wrenched his head back, cutting his throat from ear to ear with a silver-handled knife. The old-looking man was clumsier, lashing out with his crutch to catch the remaining manservant behind the ear, then stabbing him as he tried to rise. Even that effort was enough that he all but collapsed, clinging to his crutch for support.

"Are you all right?" the woman asked.

"I'll be fine," the man started to say. "I'm just embarrassed. I should be able to take two like that without even—"

"I was asking *her*, Renard," she said, looking at Orianne and offering her a hand.

Orianne took it, letting the other woman help her to her feet. She cut the bonds holding Orianne's wrists with a single sweep of her knife.

"I... I think I'm all right," Orianne said. "I... know you, don't I? From court?"

The other woman nodded. "I'm Aurelle. And I know you. You used to visit Meredith at the House of Sighs. You're Orianne, the one who works for Princess Lenore."

Orianne nodded.

"This is Renard," Aurelle said with a gesture toward the man.

"Thank you," Orianne said. "You saved my life. You both did."

Aurelle looked uncomfortable, as if she wasn't used to being thanked for that kind of thing, or maybe as if she thought she didn't deserve it.

"What are you even doing out here?" she asked.

"They brought me out here to kill me," Orianne said, and the shock of that hit her in a rush. Before, she hadn't thought about it, but now, she felt her legs going weak. Renard put out a hand to steady her, but then Aurelle had to steady him in turn, so that it seemed for a moment as if they were all holding one another up.

"You're safe now," Aurelle said. "They're dead. They can't hurt anyone anymore."

Orianne nodded.

"You should probably find somewhere to run to," Renard said. "We need to go to Royalsport, but you—"

"I need to go back to Royalsport too," Orianne said. "The men... they said that there was going to be an attempt to kill Lenore, and that the city had been taken by the Southerners. If all that's true, she'll need my help. Can I... can I go there with you?"

"We're off about dangerous quests," Renard said. "It might be dangerous to be around us."

"More dangerous than having men try to murder me in the forest?" Orianne asked.

Aurelle put a hand on her shoulder. "We can travel together, for now. Renard, remember that of the three of us, *you're* probably the weakest in a fight right now."

"I have defeated dragons. I have defeated the Hidden themselves."

"You've *run away* from them. It's not quite the same." She turned her attention back to Orianne. "We'll get back into the city together, if we can find a way."

Orianne had an idea for that. "We came here by cart," she said. "If we take their uniforms, and ride it, they'll let us in, I think. They said something about Finnal having done a deal with King Ravin."

"Finnal?" Aurelle said, her eyes hardening. "These were his men?"

Orianne nodded.

"Then this could be everything I need," Aurelle said. "Come on, we need to get going. I have a task to perform, and Renard needs to find a sorcerer, and you—"

"I have to get back there in time to stop Lenore from dying," Orianne finished for her.

Chapter Thirty Two

One of the skills Anders' tutors had taught him was the knack of using seeing to track someone. They'd shown him a dozen ways to do it, with cards or knuckle bones, flames or mirrors. One thing they all had in common was focusing the mind on a person, forming a connection with magic, letting the distraction of an object take away the outside world long enough to find a way to them.

For now, Anders was using fire, watching the flickering of his campfire while he concentrated on the boy who had stolen the shards that should have been his. Who had stolen more than that: he'd taken Anders' destiny. Anders had a name for him, and he knew what he carried with him. It was the beginning of a connection.

There was more, though. If this boy was supposed to be another collecting the shards, if he had the same *destiny* as Anders, then that was already a powerful connection. It didn't take much to build that connection with the magic inside him, and link that to the complexity of the flames.

He watched as they turned against the direction of the wind, flickering as surely as a pointing sign. Anders damped down the flames, packed up his camp, and set off in the direction they'd indicated.

For the longest time, there was only the walking, fueled by his anger at what he had lost, both his destiny and his friends. He walked until his muscles ached, over open fields and broken, stony ground. He crossed a stream on foot when he couldn't find a bridge and ignored the cold for half a league before he stopped to make another fire in the shelter of an ancient oak that curved up over him, almost devoid of leaves.

It took time to light a fire, because a light smattering of rain was start-ing to fall, and eventually, Anders gave in to his annoyance, using his magic to form the smallest of embers. He narrowed his focus down to a single furious point, and even if the effort of it was enough to make him sweat, Anders quickly had a fire blazing.

"You've been taught better than that, Anders."

Anders looked up at the sound of Master Grey's voice. The old man stood across from him on the other side of the fire, and Anders' first instinct was to lunge at him to drive a blade through his chest. Anders knew a sending when he saw one, though, and knew that if he tried it, he would only pass straight through the image, looking even more fool-ish than he had each time he'd reached the empty spot where a shard should be.

"To just force magic, rather than balancing all the factors?" Master Grey said. "It's sloppy."

"Don't lecture me, sorcerer," Anders said, glaring at the old man's image. He was as bald and inscrutable as ever. "Not after all you've done."

"And what have I done?" Master Grey said.

Anders' fury rose up then. "What have you done? You've manipu-lated me my whole life. You lied to me. You told me that it was my destiny to find the shards of the unfinished blade. I've spent my whole life prepar-ing for it, but all I've found are empty spaces."

Master Grey's image gave the impression of sitting down opposite him, on the far side of the fire.

"You still have an important destiny, my boy," he said. "You have a crucial role to play in the things that are to come."

"Why?" Anders demanded. "Because you say so? Because you've manipulated everything so that I will? You spend so much of your life talk-ing about balancing all the factors so that the smallest touch can change things. Is that all I am? Am I just one small factor, among all the rest of it?"

He saw Master Grey try for a soothing expression. He wasn't very good at it.

"You know that you have a crucial role to play," the magus said. "You know that your destiny requires that—"

"My destiny, or Devin's?" Anders shouted back at him.

That got the old man to shut up for a moment, just staring at him.

"Yes, I know about him," Anders said. "The other one you sent to do this. The one who beat me to all the shards. What was I? The backup? The one you sent out in case your *preferred* option failed?"

Master Grey shook his head. "That's not what it was at all."

"Then what?" Anders said. "Give me another explanation."

But of course, Master Grey didn't deal in explanations. The magus dealt in half-truths and total lies, treating people as if they were pieces of a puzzle, to be moved around until he liked the shape of it.

"I have felt your magic," Master Grey said, with a pointed look toward the fire. "I knew you were searching for something, but I wasn't sure what. You're looking for Devin, aren't you?"

"And I'll find him," Anders said. "Him, and the shards. I'm going to take back what should be mine."

Master Grey's eyes widened at that. "Do not do that."

"Why shouldn't I?" Anders snarled. He stood and he drew his sword, even though he knew it wouldn't do any good directly. "I have spent my life preparing for this!"

"So did he," Master Grey said. "Although he did not know it. You, at least, had the benefits of an education in magic and combat. He had a job at the House of Weapons, and what he could learn by watching."

So he wasn't even as skilled as Anders? That didn't help Anders' mood.

"I've lost *friends* on this journey!"

"So did he," Master Grey replied. "Knights of the Spur died to get him where he needed to be."

"You're talking as if he and I are somehow the same," Anders said. "As if we're *equals*."

"You're more than that," Master Grey said. "You are both essential."

"You'd better hope he isn't *too* essential," Anders snapped, "because when I find this boy of yours, I'm going to drive a blade down his throat for all the things he's cost me."

"You *cannot!*" Master Grey insisted, sounding shocked that Anders would even suggest it. Anders found himself pleased by that. It was good that *something* could scratch the surface of the old liar's equanimity. "Anders, listen to me, you and Devin are two sides of the same coin, bound together in your destiny, both as crucial as one another. The things that are to follow require both of you. If you were to kill him, it would bring disaster!"

The panic in his voice was almost enough to convince Anders, because the sheer strength of the reaction was like nothing Master Grey had shown around him before. That thought, though, brought with it others.

"Tell me, Sorcerer, would you be reacting the same way if it were *me* in danger?" Anders demanded.

"You are just as important a part of the things that follow, Anders," Master Grey replied.

The problem was simple though: Anders didn't believe him. Anders had met the sorcerer plenty of times before, but he'd never reacted with that kind of concern. He was here now to try to stop Anders from hurting his favorite, but he hadn't been there to interfere any of the times Anders had been in danger, hadn't been there to save the lives of Anders' friends.

"Not yet," Anders said, "but I will be. If this 'Devin' is dead, I can have my destiny back. I can be the man you told me I was always meant to be."

"Anders, no!" Master Grey said.

Anders struck out with his sword, plunging it into the image Master Grey was sending. He couldn't hope to hurt the magus like that, but there were things that he *could* do. He took the disruption that the sword's passage caused, and built on it, sowing chaos in the image, splintering it like a mirror so that it fell away into shards.

Anders sheathed his sword and kicked his fire down so that it fell to nothing. It was time to move on again. It didn't matter that his legs hadn't dried out yet; his anger would keep him warm. Some of that anger was at Master Grey for all the ways the old man had manipulated him throughout his life. He reserved more of it for himself, for not seeing the truth of all this earlier.

Strangely, he didn't feel angry now toward this other boy, this "Devin," who was obviously the one Master Grey *wanted* to succeed. Instead, Anders only felt the cold certainty of what he had to do when it came to him. Anders didn't believe that nonsense about them being two halves of a whole even for a moment; it was obviously just a way to try to persuade Anders to leave Devin alive.

That wasn't going to happen.

Anders would find him, and if what the magus had said was true, he would find a boy who didn't have his well-trained skills in war and in magic. He would find a boy who wasn't worthy of being the one to fulfill the destiny that had been set out, and who didn't have a chance of stopping him from taking the shards that should have been his in the first place. Anders was going to kill him, take the shards, and go back to being the one who had been chosen for this.

There was only room for one to be the lynchpin of the things that were to come, and Anders was determined that it would be him, even if that meant burying a blade in this Devin's heart.

Chapter Thirty Three

A ethe followed Ravin through the castle at a discreet distance, following the purple swirl of his robes as he rounded corners and descended staircases. She could feel her anticipation building as she waited, her thoughts racing over all the ways that this might go.

It was hard, dangerous work, planning a coup.

Aethe followed Ravin through one of the castle's halls, where servants were working to raise his trophies and set out pictures depicting his triumphs. A pile of helms from different corners of his empire represented all of the peoples he'd conquered in bringing the Southern Kingdom together. There was an arrogance to it that made Aethe sick with hatred, but it also gave her hope. Ravin was the thing holding all this together. With him gone each of those fragments would go its own way.

At least, with the right encouragement. As she stood there in the shadow of a suit of gilded armor, Aethe thought about all the people she'd had to talk to in the last few days, all the small conversations, the hints, the threats and the outright begging. It was amazing how easily the small intrigues of a life at court could prepare her for this moment.

She'd talked to nobles loyal to her husband, reminding them of their glory days on the battlefield. She'd talked to soldiers, reminding them of their duties. She'd planned who would strike where, coordinating each step of this quietly,

She'd talked to men among Ravin's forces, not *suggesting* anything exactly, but just reminding them of their old rivalries. She'd pointed out a man cheating at cards, the way the Quiet Men were hated by all, the way the city dwellers thought themselves so much better than the tribesmen or the peasant folk.

Ravin was moving on now, his back to Aethe, heading in the direction of the castle's library. The arrogance of the man was incredible, walking the castle without guards. It would be so easy to just step up to him and put a knife in his back, so easy to just...

Not yet. The plan required so much more than that.

To kill Ravin without the rest of it would be stupid. His troops controlled the city, the *country*, or at least enough of it that it didn't make any difference what was left. The moment he died, others would step into the vacuum, and their revenge would be terrible. There were others who needed to die in the same moment, so that they could take control of the city, and so that there would be no obvious successor. Then, the Southerners would fall into fighting among themselves, and it would be easy to take the kingdom again.

That was why Aethe had coordinated everything. At noon, the bells of the House of Scholars would sound. At that moment, all of the elements that Aethe had so carefully planned would come together in a hundred small strikes that didn't even need sword-wielding knights. The Southerners allowed them only daggers, but daggers would be enough for this.

She just had to wait, and not for much longer, because the sun was already growing high in the sky. She followed Ravin into the castle's library, watching as he perused the books that Greave used to love so much. It seemed strange, watching someone so cruel touch them, after someone so gentle. Aethe pressed herself back behind a shelf as Ravin left, following a few paces behind until she was sure he was heading to the great hall.

She angled off and moved to the spot where the other part of her plan would come into play, going to the passage through which Ravin's men had gained entry. There were guards on it, but one of the servants was already offering them the drink Aethe had told her to. The two men clutched at their throats, then fell.

"You've done well," Aethe said to the girl. "Go and stay safe. This will be done soon."

She opened the doorway, creating a gap through which the men waiting beyond could enter. They were a mix of soldiers from out in the city and tough men who had worked in the House of Weapons before all this.

There were only a couple of dozen of them here, but it was more than enough for what Aethe needed.

"Where are the bells?" one asked.

"They'll come," Aethe said. The sun was high enough that it would be only moments now. "We need to do this *now*."

She rushed forward, the excitement of the moment powering her steps. The men around her moved in a tight knot. They knew what their job was, and each man there looked determined to do it. They headed for the great hall as a mass, plunging down the passages of the castle. A guardsman got in the way, and their group rolled over him, one of the soldiers plunging a sword through his heart without even stopping.

They reached the doors to the great hall, and it was empty except for Ravin, sitting on his throne, a couple of guards beside him. Aethe stepped in, savoring the moment, wanting to be able to enjoy this in the time to come.

"Now!" Aethe yelled.

Aethe's men rushed into the space, and they cut the guards down even as they tried to move to fight.

Aethe moved to Ravin in that moment, making sure that she reached him before the rest of them could. She thrust with her dagger, up into his heart, feeling the sensation of the blade pushing through flesh, and the satisfaction as she looked into his eyes. She watched him die, watched the breath leaving his body, and she wished that she could do this a thousand more times.

"This is for my husband, and my daughters, and my *kingdom*," she snarled at him.

There was a hint of satisfaction in doing this, but it wasn't enough, wasn't nearly enough to make up for the things Ravin had done. She could kill him again and again, and it wouldn't be enough to make her feel better.

Aethe stood there in the silence that followed, breathing hard in her satisfaction. She'd done it. She'd actually slain the butcher who had taken her husband from her. She looked down at his corpse, not wanting to think about what would come next for a second, wanting just to sink into this.

Slowly, Aethe started to drift out of the moment. She knew she had to think about the next thing, and the next. This was no time to top. She looked around at her men, thinking about the small fights that would be taking place around the city, that would...

Where were the bells?

One sound came through the silence: the sound of someone clapping, slowly and deliberately. A figure stepped in, and for a moment Aethe could only stare as King Ravin stood there, clad in his armor, powerful and very much alive.

"It's amazing what a man will do for his family, isn't it?" Ravin said. "I told this one that if he didn't do what I required, I would kill all of them while he watched, but that if he did, they would be rewarded. All of that, because he has enough of a resemblance to fool a northerner blinded by her hate."

Aethe started to rush forward, but soldiers rushed in around Ravin then, pouring in to fill the room and surround her men.

"It doesn't matter," she said. "It doesn't matter if you kill me. All around the city, your people are dying. If I put one knife in you..."

"Where are your precious bells?" Ravin asked. Those words cut through even Aethe's determination. She stopped, listening.

"Do you think that I believed your submission?" Ravin said. "That I wouldn't have my Quiet Men notice who you met with, or where they went? Around the city, knives have been stopped in their sheaths, men pulled into quiet corners before they can strike. I only let it go this far because I wanted to see if you truly had the strength to kill me."

Fury and desperation blurred together in Aethe then. She lunged forward, stabbing with the dagger that she held, but it only broke as it struck the scales of Ravin's armor. The shards of the blade fell to the floor, and Ravin shoved her back as casually as he might have a child.

He gestured, and his men shoved someone forward. Aethe recognized the servant who had helped her. Even as Aethe stared in horror, Ravin drew his sword and struck in one movement, the tip of the great sword appearing through the girl's throat. He drew it back, and the girl crumpled, collapsing to the ground with a look of agony on her face as she died.

Aethe went to the servant, holding her hand. "You didn't have to do that."

"I didn't," Ravin said. "*You* did that. You killed her the moment that you involved her in your plot, the way that you've killed so many others. All the men here, for a start."

Aethe stood, a flash of determination running through her. "Then why shouldn't I order these men to charge? Why shouldn't we at least kill you?"

Ravin nodded to the spot where his double's corpse lay. "For the same reason he let you kill him: family. At the moment, you will die. Give the order, and you will watch your daughters flayed to death first. Any man who tries to fight will watch all those he loves tortured to death before his own demise, and that will be a thing off horror people will talk about for the rest of time. Those who surrender will be given a swift death, almost painless."

Aethe swallowed at those words. Out in the city square, when she'd knelt to Ravin, she'd thought that she was outwitting him, letting him think that he'd won. Now, he *had* won. There was nothing else she could do, no trick she could try, no coming back from this.

She fell to her knees, letting the hilt of her dagger clatter to the ground. Around her, she heard the rattle of other weapons falling against the floor of the great hall, men dropping to their knees, one by one, until eventually, they were all disarmed. Ravin's men rushed in to bind them, and Aethe stared up at him with hatred.

"Don't worry," Ravin said. "I'm not going to kill you now. I want it to be far more of a spectacle than that."

Chapter Thirty Four

Vars spent his morning trying to ignore the insults heaped upon him, and failing. The new emperor had him trailing in his wake like some kind of dog, and now, as it neared noon, Vars wasn't sure that he could stand it much longer. Except that he had to, because he knew that the moment he tried to argue with any of it, he would be slain.

Ravin sat in his new chambers, calm and silent, wearing his armor even though there seemed to be no reason for him to do so. *Emperor* Ravin, Vars corrected himself, because Vars didn't dare forget that even in his thoughts.

Vars stood to one side. Vars wasn't the only other one there, because soldiers stood around the room, looking as though they were ready for a battle. Two guards stood next to Vars, ostensibly for his defense, but he knew that they were as much his jailors as his protectors.

For the moment, he seemed to be looking over papers that could have been reports or messages declaring loyalty, communications from the south, or just the scribblings of people eager to please him. Vars had briefly had that kind of thing to look over, back when he'd been a real king, and not this joke of one.

"Is there something wrong, King Vars?" Ravin said, without looking up from his paperwork.

Vars almost didn't say anything, but he knew that would just leave him as what he was. "I could help you."

Emperor Ravin didn't look up.

"I said that I could help you," Vars said. "I know how much there is to do as a king, and I could help to do it. I know how to command, and how to make things happen."

"Do you?" Now Ravin looked his way.

"All I'm saying is that you've allowed Finnal and Duke Viris to do things for you. They'll rule their own lands on your behalf, actually make decisions, and it will make your life easier."

He saw Ravin cock his head to one side. "You're saying that you will help me? How?"

"I've just told you," Vars said. "I could help to run things here. I could—"

"Do you know why I didn't kill you?" Ravin said.

Vars felt fear shoot through him at the thought of that. "You said, because I helped you, that—"

"I don't mean when I took the city," Ravin said. "I mean before that. Why did I let you live? I arranged to distract and kill your brother, because he could have led some brave act that might have struck from nowhere. I celebrated your father's death, because he was an adversary who had won wars against deadly foes."

"Then you have me to thank for that," Vars said. "I was the one who—"

"I was not finished," Ravin said, cutting him off. He kept going. "When I had your sister kidnapped, it wasn't just because I wanted her, or because I wanted to lure in your brother. People might have rallied round her, because she has the charisma for that. I have sent my Quiet Men to finish the job because of that, and I'll probably kill dear Erin, because she is a fierce thing, and slowed my invasion. Had your brother Greave been here, I might have poisoned even him, for fear of what his mind might come up with. Why did I not kill you, Vars, son of Godwin?"

"I don't—"

"Because you are *useless!*" All of a sudden, Ravin was on his feet, his voice raised to bellow at Vars. "I let you live because there is nothing of value you can do, no talent that you possess. You live because you are no threat to me, and you are no threat to me because you are useless! You are a stupid little coward, who cannot command men, or inspire them, or plan two steps beyond his own feet. Now, sit there, and be grateful that you are all of those things, because they are the only reason you still breathe!"

Even while the shock of it hit Vars, Ravin was already sitting down again, as calmly as if nothing had happened. Vars wanted to say something, wanted to do something, wanted to protest that he wasn't any of those things, yet his fear held him pinned. Fear, and the simple thought that too much of what Ravin had said was true.

The new emperor spoke again, and now his voice was as calm as if he had never raised his voice.

"I will have announcements for you to make soon," Ravin said. "The execution of Queen Aethe, for one thing."

That made surprise replace everything else that Vars felt.

"She thinks that she is about to kill me," Ravin said, as he made a note on a piece of parchment using a quill. "She thinks that her people are about to rise up and overthrow me. She will fail, and you should be grateful that she will fail, because I am sure that she would kill you next if she succeeded."

A pair of guards walked in, holding a servant between them.

"Ah," Ravin said, "it seems that it is time. Wait here, King Vars. The *real* ruler has things to do."

He stood, leaving Vars open-mouthed as he walked out, accompanied by his guards as he left. Only one remained behind, standing by Vars, the contempt on his face obvious.

All the things Vars had been holding back ran through him, all at once. Shame at the contempt that Ravin had shown him, and anger that he'd thought he wasn't even worth killing. Then there was the fear; fear that seemed to overwhelm almost everything else. Vars saw what he was in that moment: a toy for Ravin to keep around until he got bored of humiliating him. At that point, Vars would be lucky if he died quickly.

Then there was Queen Aethe's supposed uprising. Vars knew his stepmother far better than Ravin did. She was not the fool that he might think. She was cunning, and dangerous, and if she had thought of a way to strike back, then there was a chance that it might even work. Ravin had been right about one thing though: if she won, Vars was dead.

He was dead either way, eventually, so what did that leave? Escape was the obvious option, but how? It would need to be carefully planned, need to be worked out to the last detail, need to be ...

Or would it?

Now, in this moment, Ravin's forces were distracted. They were busy dealing with Aethe's uprising, and whoever won, there would be enough of a struggle to create openings. Now was the moment, possibly his only chance. Vars started to walk to the door.

"Where do you think you're going?" the guard with him demanded, grabbing Vars by the shoulder.

Fear gave Vars the strength to turn back into the man, pressing close. It let him grab a knife from his belt and thrust it, once, twice, into his torso. Vars felt sick with the horror of it, sure that the other man would somehow find a way to block the attack, yet he still did it. This was what he needed to do to save his life, and he would do *anything* to do that. He held the soldier close to him, covering his mouth with his hand, until he went limp. Then Vars laid him down on the bed and stripped off his uniform.

The red in it helped to disguise the bloodstains, but it was still a long way from being perfect. Even so, Vars pulled the uniform on, knowing that he couldn't rely on the castle's secret exit now that Ravin and his men knew of it. He dragged the stupid excuse for a crown from his head, tossing it to one side with a clatter of metal on stone.

Vars set off walking through the halls of the castle, every instinct screaming at him that he was doing this wrong, that he was going to be caught, that the first person who saw him would kill him for what he'd done. The fear of staying was greater than the fear of going, though, and Vars kept walking.

He saw a guard walking down the same corridor as him, heading in Vars's direction, and it was all Vars could do to keep from darting into a room. Instead, he kept walking, keeping his head down.

"Shouldn't you be out with the others helping with the cleanup?" the guard called to him.

"Orders," Vars grunted back. "Message...about King Vars."

The other man laughed. "Him? Who cares about him? The emperor will just kill him soon anyway."

A braver man that Vars might have said something at that moment, but then, a braver man would have died for it. Vars just mumbled a response and kept walking, heading down through the castle's keep, taking staircase after staircase until he reached the doors to the outside world. The guards on them didn't even give him a second glance.

Vars walked across the castle's courtyard, certain with every step that there would be a cry behind him, maybe a crossbow bolt in the back. Just the thought of that made him squirm, made him want to throw up, or run, or both.

Somehow, he managed to keep walking, out to the castle's outer gates, past the guards there who did nothing but nod to him as he went. Only once he was past them did Vars run, down into the city. There, he would steal a horse, or stow away on a cart, or something.

It didn't matter, just so long as he was *safe*.

CHAPTER THIRTY FIVE

Devin almost welcomed the heat of the forge against the cold of the land around him as he hammered at the billet of star metal, turning it, little by little, into the sword it was meant to be. He enjoyed this, was good at it, yet even so his brow creased with the strain of the work.

The magic involved was what made it hard, even with Sigil nearby, close enough to touch. He'd managed to scribe his protective runes, but Devin had no illusions about them being perfect. He still had to focus as if any mistake would send wild energy searing out into the landscape around him, or kill him, or both. That was enough to make Devin consider each hammer blow he made, each small flicker of power he used to keep the star metal malleable in a way it would never have been otherwise.

This sword was even more difficult than the one he'd handed to Finnal as a wedding present. Part of that seemed to be that the fragments he was working with were so much purer than the ore he'd found in Clearwater Deep, so that any flash of magic ran through the metal all the quicker. Part of it was that someone had worked these fragments before, and the essences of the different energies within them fought for supremacy as Devin worked. The same discord that seemed to have fractured the blade in the first place threatened to burst it apart every time Devin sought to work it all together.

Yet somehow, he was managing it. All those years at the House of Weapons had provided him with the skills he needed to see the flaws in the metal as they started to rise, to smooth them and to prevent them from turning into cracks. Sigil's presence let him feel the magic around him more easily.

Combined with the understanding of magic he had gained on his journey, that it was not one fixed thing, but a thing almost to be learned every time it was used, Devin found that he was able to keep the billet of metal together, shape it, hone it. He worked runes into it as he went, similar to the ones on the walls, the swirls of them smoothing the energies within, making them flow together better. Each one traced an effort of Devin's will, and now he understood why an ordinary smith couldn't just have done this with Master Grey standing over him. It had to be *his* weaving, *his* own magic that he hammered into place on the blade.

Devin set the blade aside to rest, taking a drink of water. It was almost done, but with a blade like this, even wrapping the handle and setting the pommel were parts of the whole, so that either one could potentially disrupt the power within. He couldn't afford to rush this, however much he wanted to be back in Royalsport, to see Lenore again.

He stood there looking out over the open ground beyond the hamlet, and that was why he saw the boy approaching.

He looked to be Devin's age, with close-cut blond hair and broad shoulders. He was wearing dark clothes and had a sword at his side, while he carried a pack on his back that suggested he'd come a long way.

Devin made sure that he had his own sword close at hand, because he couldn't understand why a stranger would just come to this place, so far from anywhere else. The inhabitants had all been shocked enough to see *him*. Sigil moved up beside him, ears pricked.

The boy stopped a little way away, staring at Devin, and at the nearly finished sword that sat on the bench of the forge.

"You're Devin, aren't you?" he called out, stopping just short of the forge.

"Who are you?" Devin called back.

"My name's Anders," he replied. He looked over the forge again, and looked over Devin. "I'm...I have a message for you, from Princess Lenore."

That name caught Devin by surprise, so that he could only stare at the other boy.

"I've come a long way to find you," Anders said. "You're...not what I expected."

"How *did* you find me?" Devin asked.

"I asked about the boy Master Grey sent, and people told me about a boy seeking fragments of an unfinished sword," Anders said. He nodded over toward the sword on the bench. "Is that it?"

Devin held it up for him to see, and he heard the other boy give a low whistle. "Impressive."

"It's not finished yet," Devin said. "You said you had a message for me?"

He needed to hear it, if it was from Lenore. The other boy took out a folded piece of parchment, placing it on the edge of the forge, and Devin snatched it up, reading quickly, eager for any news of Lenore. As he read, though, he felt his jaw slackening.

"Royalsport has fallen? Lenore is in danger? Why didn't you tell me this?" Devin demanded.

"She wanted you to read it for herself," Anders said.

Devin looked around the forge, knowing what he would have to do as surely as if it had been written into the very stones around him. He *had* to get to Lenore. He took up the unfinished sword, wrapping it in a length of cloth. Master Grey would probably want him to stay there and finish it, but he couldn't, not now, not with Lenore in danger.

"I have to go," Devin said. He would need to find supplies, but he could do that on the road. He didn't want to waste any more time. As it was, he only hoped that he would be able to get there in time. He looked over to Sigil. "Come on, boy. We have to get to Royalsport."

Anders didn't know why he had given Devin his real name. Perhaps it was because he wanted his rival to know him, at least that much, before this came to violence. Perhaps he wanted to see the other boy's reaction, to see if Master Grey had told *him* about his counterpart, the way he hadn't done with Anders.

Yet there had been no hint of recognition when Anders had said his name. That had been one of the reasons Anders hadn't killed him straight away. Another had been the wolf-like creature alongside his rival. Anders had seen the rune shape that grew in its coat, and he knew a conduit when he saw one.

The last reason had been the sword. Anders' teachers had taught him many skills, but he knew that he was no smith, not really. His plan had always been to collect the fragments and then take them back to be put together by a master smith while he put magic into them, but there had always been a faint worry at the back of Anders' mind about how well that would work.

The moment the other boy had lifted the sword for Anders to see, he'd known that it was better than anything he could have produced in the way he'd intended. He'd seen the way the metal gleamed in the light, the perfection of it. He'd seen with more than normal sight too, picking out the magic worked into the weapon. He'd also seen that it wasn't finished. *That* had helped make up Anders' mind too. If the blade had been complete, he might have killed Devin there and then, taken it and headed home. As it was, he didn't want to spend his time trying to finish something that Devin could finish for him.

Of course, that would mean following him south, all the way to Royalsport, into the danger that the message said was waiting.

Anders watched as the other boy gathered his supplies, and fetched his horse. For a moment, Anders thought about asking to travel with him, but it would take him time to find a horse for himself, and in any case, he wasn't sure that he wanted to spend too much time around the wolf thing. Some instinct said that it might be enough to sniff out what he was. No, it was better to follow on behind, so he watched as Devin rode from the hamlet, pushing his horse hard, his wolf loping along beside him with a speed with no normal wolf could manage. Anders wasn't worried about that; he knew that he could track Devin, and in any case, he knew where he was going.

Anders could see the beginnings of a plan forming in his mind. Whatever he'd said, the sorcerer had tried to arrange things so that Devin could be the one to fulfill his prophecy. Well, Anders would use that, and would use the obvious skills of the other boy in the one area where Anders was weaker. He would let Devin finish the sword for him, let him produce the blade that was supposed to be at the heart of their destiny, but Anders would be the one to wield it.

He'd never known what the threat was that he was supposed to counter, but the message he'd carried had given him that. An invasion by the Southern Kingdom was the perfect time for a hero to rise up, the moment when the kingdom needed someone with all the skills that Anders had built. Once he had the finished sword, he would wield it in defense of the kingdom, save the princess who waited in the hopes of a rescue, and rise up at the head of those who fought against King Ravin's forces.

Of course, to do that, he would need the sword, but it wouldn't be hard to take it from Devin once it was finished. Anders had seen him now, and he was sure that he would be the better fighter, the more powerful magician. If he couldn't steal the sword quietly, then it would be nothing for him to cut down Master Grey's protégé and take the weapon once and for all.

CHAPTER THIRTY SIX

Lenore could feel only anguish as she stood by her sister in the city's central square, Odd by their side, cloaks around their shoulders to disguise the armor that both Odd and Erin wore. She didn't want to be here, didn't want to watch the moment that was to follow, but the guards of the castle had given them no choice.

Were the others there by choice, the hundreds who filled the square, staring at the gallows that stood there? Had they been forced to stand and stare, and sometimes jeer, or were they doing it simply because there was a spectacle for them to watch?

There were nobles in a row before them, the ones who wanted to emphasize their continuing loyalty to Emperor Ravin. Finnal was there among them, and now it seemed that so was his father, back in the city from his estates in the country.

"I hate them," Erin said. She was leaning on her spear, disguised to look like a simple staff. "I'll kill them. I'll kill *all* of them."

Odd grasped her arm, and she shot him a look that made Lenore fear for both of them. For *all* of them. There were guards to either side of them; they couldn't afford that kind of outburst.

Emperor Ravin stood atop the gallows, hand resting on that sword of his. He looked almost happy in that moment, like he was enjoying this, like he liked the reaction of the crowd to all of this. Posts stood on the gallows, waiting.

Guards brought the prisoners down to the square in chains, and Lenore's heart broke at the sight of her mother there among them. There were bruises on the faces of some of the others there, but not on hers. The tracks of the tears were more than enough though.

She saw Erin start forward, and Odd pull her back. Erin turned toward him with a snarl on her face, but Lenore caught her other arm.

"This isn't the moment," Lenore said. "It isn't the *plan*."

The plan, the only thing they'd been able to think of in this moment. They'd been planning to escape before, and they'd only waited because her mother had told them to. Now…they could still escape, but only if they used the confusion of this moment. And that meant…that meant standing there and watching her mother *die*.

Lenore wasn't sure if she could do it, but she had to. At the very least, the guards at her back would make sure that she did.

The ones escorting her mother and the others brought them up onto the gallows. They chained them in place at the posts, hands behind them, caught in place, unable to go anywhere.

"I can't do this," Erin said. "I can't stand here like this."

"We have to," Lenore said. She knew everything that her sister had to be feeling in that moment, because she was feeling all of it herself. Did Erin think that she was the only one who could hate Ravin for what he'd done, or who wanted to change any of this?

"I can't *do* this," Erin said. She started forward, and Odd held onto her. "Let go of me. Let *go* of me, or I'll kill you!"

"No," Odd said. "You think you can fight your way through all of them? You think you can save anyone there?"

"I thought you were a fighter!" Erin snapped at him. She pulled away, but Odd held onto her, and so did Lenore. Holding Erin back was a reminder that *she* couldn't run up towards the gallows either.

Even as she struggled to hold herself back, she heard Ravin start to speak. The crowd fell silent as he did it, as if they all feared what might happen to them if they didn't do what he required.

"These ones swore fealty to me," he said, the words carrying over the murmuring of the crowd. "I am their emperor, as I am yours. Yet they sought to rise up against me. They sought to *kill* me, and that is a grievous thing. But there is a worse thing, for them: they failed."

Lenore watched the men and women on the gallows, seeing the fear in them at what was going to follow. She watched her mother, and her mother looked less scared than they did on the surface, but Lenore could see the way she was hiding it beneath her determination. She hated seeing her mother that way, hated all of it. She wanted to look away, wanted to *walk* away.

Even so, she had to watch.

"For their crimes," Ravin said. "These ones have been condemned to death. Some did not rise up directly. Some only sought to help, but it does not matter; all will die."

He raised a hand, and guards slid in behind the prisoners there; all except her mother. They slid cords of rough leather around their throats. Lenore felt as if she could feel one slipping around her own neck.

Then Ravin closed his fist, and the strangling ropes tightened.

"No," Lenore murmured, as the men and women there started to kick and struggle. But there was worse; Ravin was lifting his sword.

"Have you anything to say, Queen Aethe of the Northern Kingdom?" he demanded.

"Only that killing me stops nothing," Lenore's mother said. "You think we will be the last to rise up against you? The Northern Kingdom will never stop fighting, never rest until it is free again. All of you watching, remember this: you are stronger than you think, strong enough to rise up, strong enough to keep us all free."

Lenore stared at her mother as she said those words, feeling the weight of them sinking into her even through the grief and the horror. She wanted to go to her mother, reach out to her, help her.

Ravin and his blade gave her no chance.

He thrust it in a single movement through her mother's chest, far enough that Lenore thought she heard it embed itself in the wood beyond. Lenore cried out at that, feeling tears falling down her cheeks, pain shooting through her heart as if *she'd* been the one who was stabbed. Erin started forward again, and Lenore could see Odd holding onto her, holding her back as the crowd roared its response to the moment.

Lenore wanted to collapse there, to give into her pain, to let it overwhelm her. It felt as though there had been nothing *but* pain in her life recently, though, so that there was no space left for it inside her, so that the attempt to fit more in only squashed it down, compacted it, turned it into something harder.

"Erin," Odd said. "No."

"No?" Erin said. "You don't get to tell me no."

Lenore turned to her sister. "There's a plan. I know it's hard. I know everything you're feeling right now, but you've done your own thing once already. This time, you need to stick to the plan. We need to stick to it."

"Stick to the plan?" Erin shot back. "Our mother dies and that's all you can say?"

Lenore looked over to her. "It's what needs to happen. Now."

"Now?" Erin said, sounding as if the word wasn't sinking in.

Lenore nodded. "Now."

A flash of feral joy crossed her face, and then she and Odd turned as one, each moving to one of the guards beside Lenore, striking at the same time. They thrust quickly with their knives, bringing down the guards in a concerted movement, covered by the roaring of the crowd.

They pushed their way past the people nearest to them, letting the cries and the chaos at the sight of the dead men only add to the things covering their escape.

Now was the moment when their plan was supposed to be simple: just pull up their hoods, walk away into the chaos of the crowd, and never come back. Odd already had the hood of his cloak up around his features, looking more like a monk than ever. He was pulling Erin's up around her, forcing her to go along with it.

Lenore knew that she should do the same. This was the moment for them all to simply disappear, before Ravin's men caught on to what was happening. She knew that there was nothing left for her here. Finnal didn't care for her; he never had. She should flee Royalsport and head somewhere in the far north where she could live out her life. Maybe she could even find Devin out there somewhere, and...

...and what? Let all of this go? Let Ravin win? Let him get away with all the pain he'd caused her family, and the kingdom? Just because she didn't share Erin's wildness, that didn't mean that Lenore wanted Ravin to rule any more than her sister did.

Before, she had felt like a broken thing; something weak, without the strength to act. Now, it felt as though her grief had hardened into something more, into a fierce determination that would see Ravin fall, whatever it took.

The first thing it took was walking away, the same way that they'd planned. That was as hard as anything else Lenore had done in her life, but she did it. She did it with one hand clamped to Erin's arm to make sure her sister didn't throw herself at Ravin's men.

"We'll defeat them," Lenore promised her as they walked. "But to do that, we need to be alive."

"That isn't the plan," Odd said, as he pushed a way for them through the crowd. "The plan was that we would find our way out of the city, head out into the countryside, keep out of sight."

Lenore stepped in front of him, letting him see her features beneath the hood, letting him see her determination.

"The plan has changed."

Epilogue

Master Grey walked through the entrance to the ancient temple, feet padding softly along the floor with the ease of memory. His hands found the spots that needed to be touched to disarm the traps there, and he touched them one after another. He was careful about that; it had been a long time since he was last there, and he didn't want to get any of this wrong.

He was tired, and not just from the journeying involved in getting here. He had been using a lot of power recently, and even for a magus who understood the balance of things as well as he did, there was still an effort involved.

Regrets washed through him along with the tiredness as he walked through the temple, taking in the dragon motifs, moving past the sarcophagi and thinking of all those who had died in conflicts both recent and long forgotten. He wished that there had been more he could do, but there were limits to even his power; he could not control all things.

Take Anders as an example. Grey had not considered the way the boy might react, or the things that he might do. If he hadn't needed to focus on this part of things, Grey might have sent another image to find him, or traveled to him in person. The damage that the boy could do might be incalculable.

His current task, though, was an even more vital one. It was one that no one else might understand, but only because no one else truly understood the scope of what was about to happen. They still thought in terms of the war against the south, when the truth was that there was a far greater war waiting to be fought; a war that would pit the whole of humanity against its most ancient enemies, the masters it had cast off so long ago.

Master Grey went through into the main chamber, and saw that the roof had collapsed. He could see the marks of dragon claws around the door beyond, too, and for a moment those caused him a flicker of concern, but there was no dragon that could fit through that door, none that could take what lay beyond.

This was the safest place in the known world for his prize, protected by...

...why was the doorway open, when it had been closed when Grey had left here, so long ago? He all but ran over to it, thinking of all those who might want power such as this, from the dragons themselves to twisted things like the Hidden. Why hadn't he wiped them out long before?

Master Grey ran into the protected space of the sanctuary, ignoring the dragon friezes and statues, the tombs and the likenesses of former warriors. He had eyes only for the space at the end of the room, the space where there should have been an amulet sitting there, eight-sided and powerful, too dangerous to hold. Master Grey cried out at the sight of it, his power echoing out around the place, uncontrolled for the first time in as long as he could remember.

The space was empty.

NOW AVAILABLE FOR PRE-ORDER!

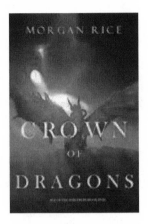

CROWN OF DRAGONS
(Age of the Sorcerers—Book Five)

"Has all the ingredients for an instant success: plots, counterplots, mystery, valiant knights, and blossoming relationships replete with broken hearts, deception and betrayal. It will keep you entertained for hours, and will satisfy all ages. Recommended for the permanent library of all fantasy readers."

—Books and Movie Reviews, Roberto Mattos (re *The Sorcerer's Ring*)

"The beginnings of something remarkable are there."

—San Francisco Book Review (re *A Quest of Heroes*)

From #1 bestseller Morgan Rice, author of *A Quest of Heroes* (over 1,300 five star reviews) comes a startlingly new fantasy series.

CROWN OF DRAGONS is book #5 in bestselling author Morgan Rice's new epic fantasy series, *Age of the Sorcerers*, which begins with book #1 (THRONE OF DRAGONS), a #1 bestseller with dozens of five-star reviews—and a free download!

In CROWN OF DRAGONS (Age of the Sorcerers—Book Five), Ravin has finally taken complete control of the capital, crushing all those in his way and subjecting its citizens to slavery and brutality.

Yet not everyone is under Ravin's thumb: Lenore, finally jolted out of her despondent state by the death of her mother, realizes it is time to step into her destiny. Instead of allowing herself to become Ravin's plaything, she must, she realizes, summon an army to defeat him.

But can she?

Devin, meanwhile, is getting closer to completing the unfinished sword and being able to return to the capital in time to help save it. Will he?

But will none of it matter if Nerra rises up, and if her dragons destroy them all?

AGE OF THE SORCERERS weaves an epic sage of love, of passion, of sibling rivalry; of rogues and hidden treasure; of monks and warriors; of honor and glory, and of betrayal, fate and destiny. It is a tale you will not put down until the early hours, one that will transport you to another world and have you fall in in love with characters you will never forget. It appeals to all ages and genders.

Book #6 will be available soon.

"A spirited fantasy....Only the beginning of what promises to be an epic young adult series."

—Midwest Book Review (re *A Quest of Heroes*)

"Action-packed.... Rice's writing is solid and the premise intriguing."
—Publishers Weekly (re *A Quest of Heroes*)

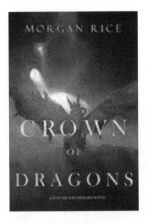

CROWN OF DRAGONS
(Age of the Sorcerers—Book Five)

Did you know that I've written multiple series? If you haven't read all my series, click the image below to download a series starter!

Made in the USA
Middletown, DE
13 December 2020